WITCHES COPSE

MATH BIRD

MCSNOWELL BOOKS

Copyright © 2023 by Math Bird

All rights reserved.

This book is a work of fiction. Names, characters, places, and incidents are the product of the author's imagination or are used fictitiously. Any resemblance to actual events, places, or persons, living or dead, is entirely coincidental.

No part of this book may be reproduced in any form or by any electronic or mechanical means, including information storage and retrieval systems, without written permission from the author, except for the use of brief quotations in a book review.

For Yan.

What is the land without a queen to reign and a worm to serve and turn the earth?

PART I

THE WINTER OF DISCONTENT

JANUARY 1979

1

Dates was studying her reflection in the bar mirror when the kid handed her the note. She gave him a fistful of change, then resumed contemplating the age of the world-weary face gawking back at her. The dim lighting helped, obscuring the blotches across her cheeks and paling the tiny veins on her nose. Slapped-on foundation did nothing to enhance her skin, and those bags under her eyes bore testament to her lack of sleep. Her body ached, and her ash-blonde hair looked grey, fitting ailments for these long, dark winter months.

Her hair hung greasy and lank, and the way it parted in the centre drew attention to her high forehead. There was some consolation at least: the vigour of a woman in her early thirties still burned through her brown eyes. She wasn't over the hill yet. But she only had to glance around this dive to realize she wasn't too far from its peak.

Despising herself took less effort in the cold. Like the rest of London, she'd sought solace in warmer climes, wasting her days in Maggie's Bar downing double whiskies followed by lager chasers. But drink only dulled the pain. The image of that poor girl lying comatose in the hospital bed harried her waking hours–tormented her in those rare moments of sleep.

Dates concentrated on the note. The handwriting looked elegant and looped, but without her glasses, the words remained a mystery. She hadn't worn them for days. She never did during spells of markedly low self-esteem, a habit she formed as a kid. Dates rubbed her eyes, sighed, and then nodded at Carrie behind the bar. Carrie was the best of a bad bunch; she always wore a smile and never made you feel you were asking for the earth whenever you bought a drink. 'Usual, Dates?' she said.

Dates shook her head. 'Nah, just an orange juice. I've decided to come off it for a few weeks.'

'What's wrong? Need a clear head?'

'Something like that.' Dates placed the note on the bar. 'Left my specs somewhere. Be a love and tell me what it says.'

Carrie held the note up to the light. 'Some bloke called Quinby wants you to come to his place in Lyall Street at eight, mentions something about a job.' She handed back the note and then popped open a bottle of orange juice. Approval flashed in her blue eyes. 'Belgravia, huh. Looks like you're going up in the world, Dates.'

Dates drank her orange juice in one thirst-laden gulp, then wiped the residue from her lips. 'Stranger things have happened, Carrie.' She glanced around the bar. 'No disrespect to Maggie, God rest her soul, but anything's a step up from this place.'

Dates slipped off her stool and headed for the Ladies, pausing before reaching the door as some beer-bellied dolt, seated at the nearby table, grunted something about her 'needing the Gents.'

She fixed the man with a stare. 'Sorry, friend. I didn't quite catch that.'

The man grinned at her. 'Jesus, it's a bird.' He looked at his friends and laughed. 'I could have sworn it was a bloke.' He gave a nonchalant shrug. 'Easy mistake to make. I suppose your hips and legs aren't bad; it's a shame you're so flat-chested.' He scanned her with a disdainful eye. 'That's a man's suit, isn't it? I wouldn't dress that way if I were you, love; believe me, it does you no favours.'

Dates grabbed a fistful of his hair, yanked his head back, and then slammed his face down on the table. One of his pals stood up, but Dates knocked him to the floor with a swift, hard kick to the crotch.

'The bitch broke my nose,' hollered the man through a mask of blood, so Dates slammed his face down again to shut him up.

Carrie rushed out from behind the bar and, with her back to Dates, pressed her towards the wall. 'Enough,' Carrie yelled.

Dates held her hands above her head. 'I was minding my own business. This man started it.'

'Well, you sure as hell finished it.'

'He needs to learn some manners. He can't speak to people like that and expect to get away with it.'

Carrie ushered Dates towards the door. 'I think you've made that clear, don't you?' She rested a hand on Dates's shoulder. 'Go and see about that job and stay out of here for a few weeks.' She nodded towards the men's table. 'That crowd bears a grudge. I'd keep a low profile if I were you.'

2

Dates got the tube to Sloane Square, then walked the rest of the way. The refuse collectors had been striking for weeks, and bin bags and rotten food lined the London alleyways and streets. The January air reeked of neglect, making the winter of '79 the perfect place for self-loathing.

On reaching Quinby's large townhouse, Dates took one last drag of her cigarette and then stubbed it out, placing it in her pocket for later. Although Quinby's reputation frightened most people, Dates never felt nervous in his company. She took him seriously, of course. For all his oddities, Quinby provided legal counsel for most of the dangerous villains in town. People owed him favours; he had connections, two vital ingredients to warrant respect.

She rang the doorbell, stepping back as one of Quinby's young male friends opened the door. 'Yes?' he said, with a patronizing air.

'I'm here to see Quinby.'

'And you are, Sir?'

Dates rolled her eyes. 'Ms Elizabeth May Daton, just tell him it's *Dates*.'

The young man gave Dates a disdainful look and, without answering, led her into a large room that he referred to as the *library*. 'Wait here, please, *Ms* Daton. Quentin will be with you shortly.'

The room was wall-to-wall books, ancient-looking texts, leather-bound in various shades of brown, in harmony with the towering oak bookcases that housed them. The glazed, twelve-panelled oak display cases in the room's centre drew her closer. Mounted on a table base, each case contained an assortment of what she could only describe as antiquated scientific instruments: brass microscopes, sextants, compasses and sundials, a collection you'd expect from a man of Quinby's ilk.

Stories about Quinby ran rife. How he enjoyed spiking drinks and had a penchant for young men. Someone once told her he practised black magic, worshipped Satan, and even owned a collection of shrunken heads. Dates made a joke of it at the time, but the part of her, which knew about the darkness a man like Quinby was capable of, took such rumours seriously.

God knows what lay within those books. Perhaps the wooden carving above the fireplace, portraying a young woman hanging lifelessly from a tree with two small demons perched on each shoulder, told her everything she needed to know.

Sensing a presence behind her, Dates turned around, trying not to react to the amused look on Quinby's face.

'Never thought you as an appreciator of the arts, Dates,' he said, closing the door behind him. He pointed at one of two red velvet chairs placed on either side of a small table. 'Please, sit, and I'll fix us both a drink.' Dates almost told him she'd quit, but, seeing as he owned an extensive stock of vintage Malts, thought, *what the hell*.

She sat in the chair as directed, and after passing her a

drink, Quinby sat in the chair opposite. Dates took a sip, momentarily closing her eyes while savouring the taste. She shivered slightly and stared uneasily at the open window. That amused look returned to Quinby's face. 'You know, I find having a cold shower every few hours makes this cursed weather more tolerable. You feel more benefit when you're indoors, although looking at the state of you, once a week would be a tremendous improvement.'

Dates sipped her whisky. 'A long bath is on the top of my list once we're done. Cold showers are for men with a guilty conscience.'

Quinby laughed. 'That's a quick response for the uneducated.' He scrutinized her for a moment. 'You know, I've always thought there's a handsome creature lurking beneath that shabby exterior. You're not as ugly as folks make out. Yes, there's something there, something behind the eyes, perhaps? You're an athletic type, although considering you are ex-military, you should take better care of yourself.'

'I had the same notion,' Dates said. 'Perhaps the money from this job will put me on the right path.'

'Perhaps, although I haven't given you the job yet. People are still talking about your last debacle.'

Dates sighed. 'That wasn't entirely my fault.'

Quinby gave her a sceptical look. 'Is that so? Have you told the young girl's parents that? She's at Great Ormond Street, so I believe. A medical acquaintance of mine said it was touch and go.'

Dates's heart thumped inside her throat. 'I'm going to help them as best I can. Once I earn some money, I'll see them right.'

'And how do you plan to achieve that,' Quinby scoffed, 'when everybody in your line of business refuses to work with you?'

'I'm resolved to put things right.'

Quinby shook his head and sighed. 'Oh, the foolishness of youth, ruined reputations seldomly redeem themselves.' He fixed her with a stare. 'Self-neglect is often more apparent in a woman. Your appearance displeases me.'

The feeling was mutual. Dates saw nothing charming in Quinby's foppish exterior. He looked too groomed, his slicked-back hair always the same length, his short back and sides razor cut to a flawless line. As usual, he wore a three-piece suit. It fitted him perfectly, complimenting his posture and mannerisms as crafted and deliberate as every painstaking cut and stitch.

Quinby sat upright, one short, spindly leg crossed over the other, a glass in one hand, the other resting uniformly across his waist, presumably to hide his gut. For all his preening, he failed to mask all the scars of overindulgence; his pale skin exaggerated his ruddy, flaccid cheeks; and the thin layer of foundation around the eyes only drew attention to the shadows that lurked beneath. Even his posh accent hid something, lapsing now and again into what Dates's tuned ear recognised as an east-end twang.

She finished her whisky, 'Sorry to be such a disappointment,' and stood up. 'Let me know should you have any more work that's suitable, something lowly for a woman of my standing. I'd never dream of trying to rise above myself.'

Quinby rolled his eyes. 'Sit down and don't be so melodramatic. You wouldn't be drinking my malt if I didn't have a use for you.' He studied her for a moment. 'You're a Cancerian, right?'

Dates nodded suspiciously. 'Birthday's June twenty-first; how did you know that?'

Quinby beamed. 'Let's say your temperament gave it away.'

Dates motioned towards the door. 'Here we go again. Listen, Quinby, perhaps it's best if you–'

'*Sit down*,' Quinby demanded. 'I meant it as a compliment.' The light reflected in Quinby's eyes. 'I envy those born on the Summer solstice; this is the perfect job for you.'

'Really,' Dates said, 'and why's that?'

Quinby scratched the side of his head and, ignoring the question, said, 'Ever been to North East Wales, Dates? It's a shit-hole of a place close to the English border.'

'I have, actually.'

'Don't tell me, let me guess, one of those ghastly holiday parks in the seaside town of Rhyl?'

'No, I worked for a travelling funfair when I was fifteen. Only lasted a summer but got to see most of the country.'

'Yes, I can imagine you doing that. Well, at least you'll know what to expect. It should stand you in good stead.' He slid a hand into his pocket, drew out a white envelope, and tossed it onto her lap. 'The place you're going to is a small village called *Ysceifiog*.' He bowed at the envelope. 'That should cover your time and expenses.'

'To do what, precisely?'

'Escort an acquaintance of mine, persuade her to return with you. You place all your special talents into achieving that, and there'll be ten times as much waiting for you when you get back. I'll spread the news if you're successful. People quickly forget when those with influence ask them to, and with the money you'll make on this, you'll be able to help that poor girl and her family.'

Dates stared longingly at the wad of notes. 'Okay,' she said without pause. 'What do I need to know?'

'They'll reveal all once you get there.'

'*They*?'

'A miscreant called Eves and his oversized partner,

Casey. They're lodging at the White Hart pub; you shouldn't have a problem getting a room.'

'The name Casey sounds familiar. If it's the guy I'm thinking of, he's a pro.'

'Yes, however, he doesn't have the constitution for this particular task.'

'What do you mean?'

'Nothing, only that it demands a more feminine touch.'

Dates quickly put the envelope in her pocket before Quinby changed his mind. Quinby stared into his glass and sighed. 'Treat them with a firm hand, Dates, and make it clear I'm losing patience.'

3

After a hot bath and a clean set of clothes, Dates drove to North East Wales in the orange Ford Cortina Quinby loaned her. It was a new Mark 4, its large windows flooding the cabin with grey light. The added visibility would have been a gift in better conditions, but it proved nothing but a hindrance in the rain. The car wouldn't have been her first choice. It was an executive's car, marketed to the middle classes and the aspirational. Despite that, it certainly knew how to shift, especially when cruising in fourth.

It took Dates just under four hours to reach the Welsh border. She spent most of that time in a daze, sweating out the booze, trying to distract herself by playing the Pentangle cassette she'd once stolen from a party. As was often the case, she fell prey to the music's whims and fancies. The song 'Light Flight' took her out of herself for a while. Sadly, it was short-lived as the wistful tones of 'Once I had a Sweetheart' reminded her of the girl and those insatiable feelings of loss.

The North East Wales outskirts looked exactly as she remembered. The power station towers and chimneys marred the horizon, petering out as a grey road lined with red brick houses snaked along the coast. As the estuary flickered into sight, Dates took a right off the road and followed a steep tarmac incline signposted the *Well Hill*. When she reached the top, she stopped and asked for directions, then took the road pointed out to her. The town, the estuary, and the factories faded gradually into the distance until she found herself besieged by trees and fields and what seemed like another country.

The White Hart pub was low-ceilinged and dimly lit, and the grim-looking oak furnishings were in keeping with the landlord's surliness. Dates wasted no time securing herself a room and then bought a much-needed drink. She stayed with the orange juice. She seldom drank on a job, and as the landlord handed over her change, she enquired about Eves and Casey.

The landlord's scowl complimented the aggrieved tone of his voice. 'You a friend of theirs?'

'More of an acquaintance.'

'Pleased to hear it. I'd keep my distance if I were you. A young woman like yourself would be wise to keep better company.' He regarded her for a moment. 'Casey's in his room, flat out. There's no waking him.'

'Heavy night?'

'He was in A&E until one o'clock this morning. The doctor prescribed some pills to calm him.'

'Sounds serious.'

The landlord sighed. 'It sounds like a pain in the arse if you ask me.'

'You don't want him here?'

'No, I don't. But business is quiet at the moment. Eves has paid until the end of the month. Tempted though I am, I can't afford to be handing out refunds.'

'Where is Eves?'

'Up at Witches Copse, I suppose.'

'*Witches*,' Dates said with a smile.

The landlord stared at her intensely. 'All superstitions spring from something true. My mother taught me never to mock things you don't understand.'

'Wise words indeed,' Dates said and, to break the awkward silence asked, 'What's he doing there exactly?'

The landlord shrugged. 'Nothing good, I imagine. It's a place I don't care to talk about. You'll need to ask him when he gets back.'

'When will that be?'

'Knowing him, it'll probably be later this evening.'

The roar in her stomach interrupted the moment's silence. 'Do you do food?'

He nodded. 'What do you want, chips, chop, a salad? I can open a tin of spam if you like?'

Although tempted to raise her glass and toast the high life, Dates opted for the Chop and Chips. 'I'll be over there,' she said, pointing to the most secluded corner she could find.

4

Dates sat in a rickety old spindle back chair, propping her elbows on the wobbly table. She'd scarcely touched her food, chain-smoking instead, glancing around this godforsaken room. Sadly, she wore her glasses so she could see everything. Brass kettles and copper pans hung from the exposed timbers, their shadows flickering across the big oak fireplace. It was an old-looking pub, congruent among the silver fields, the bare trees and the deathly silence surrounding it. It needed a spring clean, and Dates dreaded to think what her bathroom was like. She didn't want to be here. But in this weather, everywhere was the wrong place.

The young man, who the landlord referred to as Mr Eves, showed up just after eight-thirty. He was unshaven and lanky, his donkey jacket hanging over his skinny frame like an oversized black blanket. His manky faded jeans were tucked into his wellies, and his brown shoulder-length hair showed equal signs of neglect. He looked shabby and unwashed–a man after her own heart.

Eves ordered a pint of bitter and a packet of crisps, paying for it in small change.

Dates went over to the bar and stood beside him. 'Looks like someone's cracked open their piggy bank.' She slapped down a one-pound note. 'Let me get this; I don't want to rob a man of his life's savings.'

Eves looked at the landlord and shook his head. 'I thought you only had entertainment on Saturday nights, Frank? I would have come back earlier if I'd known you'd booked a comedian.' He shot her a sardonic smile. 'Nice glasses, by the way, going for the village idiot look? I'm sure it gets lots of laughs.'

She matched Eves's stare with her own. 'I'm not that funny. In fact, as Mr Quinby will testify, I can get very serious when pushed.'

Eves sipped his beer and followed her to her table without needing to be asked. They sat in silence, Frank watching them throughout, lowering his eyes whenever Dates caught his glance. Dates swallowed the last dregs of orange juice from her glass and set her hands on the table. 'So, what's going on?'

Eves gave her a baffled look. 'And you are?'

'The name's Daton; most folks call me Dates. Quinby sent me to sort things out, told me to tell you that "I'm the answer to your little problem".'

Eves studied her for a moment, the bewildered expression on his face fading. 'Well, you certainly look the part. That's a man's suit, right?'

'I'm not here to discuss my attire. Just tell me what's going on.'

He took the roll-up from behind his ear and held it between his middle fingers. 'I thought Quinby would have told you.'

'I'm asking you.' She flipped open the lid of her lighter and gave him a light. 'Quinby hasn't told me squat, although he hinted that you tend to mess up.'

Eves took a drag of his cigarette and blew the smoke into her face. He leaned back in his chair. 'What do you want to know?'

'Who I'm supposed to be bringing back? And what's wrong with Casey?'

'He's not having a good time of it at the moment,' Eves said, avoiding the first question. 'This job's taking its toll on him. He's having a nervous breakdown of sorts.'

'And what's brought that on?'

'Lots of things, drink, drugs, stress, tiredness, or maybe he's bewitched.'

Dates closed her left hand into a fist. 'Now, who's the comedian?'

'I'm not trying to be smart. There's a lot of crazy stuff going on in that man's head.'

'Because he's *bewitched*?'

'As odd as it sounds, yes. Well, at least he thinks so.'

Dates lit a cigarette, sizing up Eves with one broad glance. He was well-spoken for a criminal, his manner and accent too refined for a so-called miscreant. He looked more like a student or a work-shy academic, loafing his way through life, surviving on dole money and state grants. 'So, who's bewitched him?'

'Gwraig y Coed.'

'What?'

'Lady of the woods.'

'And who's she?'

Eves gulped his beer and then wiped the residue from his mouth. 'There are a couple of answers to that. Some say she's just a story. Others swear she's a witch. Or she's just a gipsy girl spaced out on mushrooms. But as far as you're concerned, *Dates*, she's the person you've been hired to bring back.'

'By gipsy, you mean she's from a travelling family?'

Eves sighed. 'Yes, that's right. Apologies for sounding so *derogatory*. I was told a teenage girl and her father came here a few months ago. No one's seen the dad since. But the girl decided to stay.'

Dates shook her head in both amusement and disbelief. 'It sounds like another unruly teenager to me. The father probably had enough. You know the kind of stuff kids get up to.'

'It's not that simple,' Eves said. 'I gave Quinby a heads up about this months ago. I did my research long before we came here.'

'Research? What are you, a scientist or something?'

'Archivist by trade, although I've been a researcher these last few years, sniffing out what Quinby likes to call his *Collectible Oddities*. Mostly it's red herrings in the dirt, but occasionally we find a diamond, and Quinby pays more than a fair price.'

'And that's what you've got here, a diamond?'

'I think so.'

Dates grinned. 'You're struggling with a lone girl in the woods. No wonder Quinby is so pissed off.'

'Casey usually handles stuff like that. He was doing fine until she started messing with his head.'

Dates dragged hard on her cigarette, nodding as she breathed the smoke out. 'Let's sort it then. Take me to her. I'm not forcing anyone against their will. There are lots of ways to persuade people. Let's put an end to this nonsense right now. Let's see what this young lady has to say for herself.'

'It's not that easy. I would if I knew where she was. But it's a waiting game. You need to sit it out; keep watching. She knows every part of those woods. Take today, for instance, I ....'

As Dates looked towards the noise coming from the back end of the bar, she saw Landlord-Frank with his hands raised, either trying to calm or surrender to the big guy looming over him. The guy was at least six foot six, bald on top, his big mad eyes in keeping with his thick beard and the wild tufts of black hair on either side of his head. Dates stubbed out her cigarette in the ashtray and felt for her knife, although she would need her Browning Hi-Power if the man-beast kicked off.

'Not again,' Eves said and dashed over to where the man stood. Dates was quick to follow, keeping a safe distance should she need to react.

Eves touched the man's arm. 'Hey, bud, what's wrong? Come on, Casey, let's sit down and have a drink.'

A hint of recognition flashed in Casey's eyes. He didn't seem quite sure who Eves was, but his presence seemed to soothe him. Casey's face and clothes were soaked in sweat, and he shivered now and then as though he had a fever. He stank, too, a foul blend of bad breath and BO.

Casey fixed his eyes on Eves, an urgent tone in his voice as he said, 'I need to beg her to give me another chance. I'm a disappointment to her.'

Eves guided Casey a few steps closer to their table. 'Come on, let's sit down.' He nodded at Dates. 'Our new friend here wants to buy us a drink.'

Dates didn't argue. More than happy to give the miscreants some space, she followed Landlord-Frank to the bar and ordered two pints of bitter, two whiskies, and an orange juice with plenty of ice. She watched Frank's hand shaking as he struggled to steady the glass and, lowering her voice, said, 'What the hell's all that about?'

Frank shook his head and sighed. 'He's been like that for days. Ever since he came back from those woods.'

'What happened to him?'

'God knows, yesterday he came back with a cut down his arm, went to A&E, possibly caught some infection. I warned them about *those woods*.' He stood a full pint of beer on the bar and snatched a clean empty. 'The place is a death trap at the best of times. Winter's the worst, especially in the dark nights.'

Dates nodded. 'What about this young travelling girl who lives out there? Doesn't seem to trouble her much.'

Frank paused briefly from pouring the drink and unconvincingly proclaimed, 'I know nothing about that.' He placed the second pint on the bar, remaining silent as he poured the orange juice, then the whiskies. 'That's one forty-six.'

Dates slammed down two notes. 'Have one for yourself.'

Frank put the notes in the till and then handed Dates her change. 'That's kind. But I'm all right, thanks, love.'

She gave him a suit-yourself smile, then slipped the coins into her pocket. She turned to face Eves. 'Hey, give us a hand with these.' Eves immediately stood up. He might have been an educated man, but the booze was definitely his calling.

Eves rubbed his hands. 'Whiskies as well. Not only are you a comedian, but you're also a philanthropist. You not drinking with us, Frank?'

Frank shook his head. 'I've got a wedding reception booked for Saturday night.' He glared at Eves. 'I want Casey gone by the morning. I'll pay back the difference; Getting him out of here is well worth the loss.'

Eves sighed. 'Come on, Frank. I think you need to think about this for a bit.'

'I've been giving it a lot of thought. In fact, I've thought about nothing else. Friday,' Frank said coldly. 'I've been more than reasonable. The wife just told me he has crapped on the bedroom carpet. You're lucky I don't call the police.'

'Frank–'

'Friday. You and your lady friend can go too if you don't like it.'

5

Dates sipped her orange juice, watching Casey mumbling like a fool. She felt on edge. Things were growing messier as the hours passed. At this rate, she wouldn't even be able to claim a couple of hundred on expenses. She needed to find this young woman fast and convince her that there was money to be made from this if she played along. She didn't even have to hand her over to Quinby. All he had requested was that she escort her back to London. Contractually, Dates would oblige, let the young woman show her face, and then offer her some protection.

Dates sensed Casey's glare and watched as his huge shovel-like hand passed her a crumpled piece of paper. She flashed Eves a puzzled look.

'He wants you to read it to him,' Eves said. 'It's the first riddle she sent him. He likes to hear it.'

'Riddles?'

'It's how she likes to communicate. There are loads of little cryptic messages carved in those woods.' He nodded at the piece of paper. 'Go on, read it.'

'You read it.'

Eves laughed. 'You *can* read, right? Or has Quinby

started hiring female Neanderthals?'

With the dexterity of a woman who had committed such acts so many times before, Dates slammed her glass down on the table and then thwacked the bridge of Eves's nose with the end of her lighter. 'If Neanderthal means I'm quick with my hands, then the answer's yes.'

Tears of shock flooded Eves's eyes. He pushed back his chair and cupped his hands over his nose. 'You dumb, ugly bitch. What was that for?'

'To remind you to watch your mouth and keep your voice down.'

Casey stirred, choosing to remain put the moment Dates slipped her arm under the table and pushed her High-Power into his crotch. The pistol had always been a good mediator, settling the man-beast more effectively than any pill. She threw Casey a wink. 'Seems you're not entirely stupid, after all. Welcome back to the real world.'

Casey remained silent, that distant look in his eyes returning, quickly transforming the grim look on his face back into a distracted half-smile.

Dates withdrew the pistol from Casey's crotch. 'It's nothing personal, fellas. But I'm broke, so I'm keen to get things sorted.'

Eves stood up, 'there are better ways to make a point,' and stomped into the Gents. He returned a few minutes later, dabbing the end of his nose with a wet ball of toilet paper. He sat back down in a huff, staring like a sulky kid into his drink.

Dates grabbed the paper and read it aloud. '*Find me in the months of the never-ending sun. Singular in the mother tongue. Where the elder trees grow.* What the hell does that mean?'

Eves sniffed. 'It's a message she left in the last place. Before I tracked her here.'

'The last place? Sounds like you've been tracking this young girl for some time. Where was she before?'

'Salisbury, when Quinby and his people brought her to my attention.'

'Quinby's *People*?'

'Folks, you'd probably never want to meet. Like Quinby, they're an acquired taste.'

'To your tastes?'

'Not exactly. It pays the bills. Only sometimes it takes you to places you shouldn't go.'

Dates nodded with a smile. 'So, where do we find her?'

Eves shrugged. 'All we can do is wait for her in those woods. See if we can get a sniff.'

'What makes you think she's still there?'

'Oh, she's there. Trust me, she's not finished with us yet, especially now we have you.'

Dates didn't like the implication of his words but ignored them. 'Okay, we'll go there first thing tomorrow morning.'

'Might be a long wait.'

'All day and night if we have to. The only thing troubling me is what if she doesn't want fetching back.'

Eves grinned. 'I thought we'd hired your special talents to deal with that?'

'Kidnapping's beyond my remit. You can get up to ten years for that or life if things go wrong.'

Eves glanced at Casey. 'You might feel different once you've spent more time with her.'

༄

Dates went to bed around eleven, just after Frank called last orders. Eves opted for a late drink, hoping to wangle his way back into Frank's good books. Frank appeared unimpressed, wearing the outward expression of a man whose guests had most definitely outstayed their welcome.

Dates stripped down to her vest and pants, splashing her face and body with warm water before getting into the cold bed. The room was poky and damp, the concrete-like pillows almost unbearable. She shivered beneath the musty eiderdown, the lumpy mattress kneading her back.

After warming up a little, she sat up and lit a cigarette, watching the smoke curl towards the battered old wardrobe. The room was no worse than her place down south, and she only focused on it because of the silence. She turned towards the window, watching the moonlit clouds drift across the winter sky. The scene had a calming effect, and she stubbed out her cigarette as she felt her eyes closing.

It was a fitful night's sleep. A much-needed rest riddled with strange dreams and temporary bouts of wakefulness. For weeks now, Dates had dreamt about her assailant's car skidding out of control and the fear in the young girl's eyes as it mounted the pavement. Yet tonight, instead of finding herself sitting beside the girl's hospital bed, Dates chased her through the village, the alleyways and streets strangely familiar. She followed her beyond the fields, immersing herself in the darkness of the woods. Dates approached her from a distance, growing more frustrated as she failed to make ground. In the abstracted images that followed, she caught only glimpses of the girl. It wasn't the face she knew but a shadow flitting through the trees, a murmur in the wind, a hint of something walking along the woodland's edge.

The girl carved letters into the trees, scratched symbols onto stones, and formed small, men-like figures from twigs. She arranged them in a line, standing them in the wet soil. *Where is the worm to turn the earth?* Sang the girl, each softly spoken word lingering coldly on the breeze.

6

Dates almost puked, watching Eves devour his runny eggs and bacon. She had no appetite, and today her empty stomach was no match for her morning chain of cigarettes. There was no sign of Casey, and when Dates asked where he was, Eves mumbled something about him going on ahead.

'To do what?'

Eves flashed her a mouthful of food. 'Get things ready, see if she's around, find us a good spot.'

'Do you think that's wise, letting him go alone?'

'He's persistent. You try arguing with him. See how far you get.'

Dates swallowed a yawn. 'So, what's the plan? We're just going to wander through those woods, hoping to catch sight of her?'

'It's all we can do. It's either that or go back.'

Dates yawned. 'Do you think she's still around?'

Eves shrugged. 'Let's hope so.' He regarded her for a moment, watching her closely when she yawned again. 'Are you okay, Dates? You look a bit peaky.'

'I'm fine.'

'Well, you don't look it. You look like crap if you ask me.'

'Well, I didn't.' Dates yawned again. 'Don't look at me like that. I had a restless night, that's all. Weird dreams kept waking me up.'

Eves sat up in his chair, a thoughtful look on his face. 'What did you dream about?'

'This and that,' Dates said. 'It was a long journey. My head was swimming with all kinds of stuff.' She tried to recall what the girl had whispered to her in her dreams. Fragments of her words crept into her mind: the *land*, the *rain*, the *turn of the worm*. She tried fleshing them out, giving them meaning, her heart beating faster with every futile attempt.

She looked dismissingly at Eves's plate. 'This isn't about me. So, hurry up stuffing your face; we've things to do.'

Eves stabbed his fork into two pieces of bacon, then a slice of sausage and stuffed the greasy concoction into his mouth. He chewed slowly, his sleepy eyes fixed on Dates throughout. He swallowed with an exaggerated gulp before wiping the grease from his mouth. 'You know, Dates, your lips were moving slightly before.'

'That usually happens when people speak. I thought you were educated?'

'No, you weren't talking. You were staring into space, a woman deep in thought.' He took a swig of coffee, rinsing it around his mouth before swallowing. 'My dad used to do that when he read the paper. What were you thinking about?'

Dates didn't answer, the girl's voice whispering like the cold wind among the trees.

It took them just under twenty minutes to drive to the woods, navigating the narrow lanes that cut through the fields, every blind bend made more treacherous by the tall hedgerows. The car fan was useless against the cold. An odour of wet soil and dead leaves tainted the air, the smell intensifying as they got closer to the thicket of trees.

Dates spent most of the journey distracted by the remnants of her dreams. She struggled to remember the young woman's words. The persistent whisper drowned out the sound of her inner voice like a niggling throbbing ache. It beseeched her to fulfil a promise that Dates, no matter how hard she tried, failed to remember.

They parked near the woods' entrance, Dates shivering slightly as she wiped the sweat from her brow. She could feel Eves's eyes burn into her and turned her head quickly, staring at him full-on. 'What the hell's your problem?'

He raised his hands to his chest. 'Nothing.'

'So why are you staring?'

'Just making sure you're all right. You're acting odd.'

'For the last time, I'm fine. You'll have plenty of time to worry about me when we're done.'

Thankfully, Eves didn't speak for at least twenty minutes after that. Keeping quiet as the partly frosted ground crunched beneath their feet, his breath growing harder with every step.

The morning mist drifted above the naked trees as the watchful crows cawed against the deathly silence. Never one for superstition, Dates felt a presence here, something skulking and unseen. Instinct told her that Eves felt it too. It wasn't only her words that silenced him.

It wasn't until they reached a small clearing in the trees that Eves broke his silence. He pointed at a ruinous circular tower, standing about thirty feet tall and ten feet in diameter.

'Well, this is us,' he said. He put two fingers in his mouth and whistled. 'Casey, are you in there, Casey? Hope you're not playing with yourself. There are ladies present.' He looked at Dates and grinned, the stupid look on his face fading when she didn't smile back. 'Are you there, Casey?' he shouted, 'stop messing around.' He walked to the tower's entrance, then glanced over his shoulder at Dates, indicating she should follow.

The tower's interior smelt like someone had just urinated on a fire. Placed in front of a circle of burnt wood and dead ash were two makeshift seats of rotten timber. Dates scanned the childlike writing, chalked, and scratched across the wall. 'What is this place?'

'A Mock Roman watchtower,' Eves said. 'They built it for Queen Victoria's Golden Jubilee. It's a handy place to rest.' He pointed to a line of writing. 'As you can see, she enjoys coming here.' Eves took out a notepad and pen. 'I haven't seen this one before.' He rested the pad on his arm. 'It's a pain using these blasted things, do us a favour and read it out to me; it'll be easier that way.'

Dates remained silent at first, the whispers in her head growing louder. She studied the scrawl of red letters, hemmed in by mysterious symbols, the knot in her stomach tightening as she read the words aloud. *'What is the land without a queen to reign and a worm to serve and turn the earth? I am the worm, and from this day, I serve.'*

'Thanks,' Eves said. 'Much appreciated; it's a big help to me.'

Dates turned towards Eves and frowned at the stupid smile on his face. 'What does this stuff mean?'

He stared at her for a moment, an odd look in his eyes. 'It'll take a lot of explaining. You'll find out soon enough.'

'What the hell is that supposed to mean?'

Before Eves could answer her, a gunshot cracked in the

air like the harbinger of a winter's storm. Dates reached for her Hi-Power.

'No need for that,' Eves said. 'It's only Casey.'

'Casey's got a gun?'

'Course, he's got a gun. He's in the same line of work as you.'

They stepped into the clearing and started running towards the sound of another gunshot. It appeared to be coming from the south side of the woods. Dates tried quickening her pace, which proved nearly impossible weaving between the trees.

Someone called out. 'Eves. Eves.' Casey's unmistakable demented cry, only this time his voice had more urgency. His call was unrelenting, pained, sporadically breaking into a sob.

They ran deeper into the woods, losing track of each other, eventually meeting up to find Casey leaning against a heap of cut trees. He was stripped down to his Y-fronts, cuts and scratches covering his body, his face masked with blood and dried tears.

Casey's discarded clothes hung limply among the trees. They had an eerie human-like shape, the mute witnesses of the horrors yet to come. Casey held a Glock in his right hand and some sort of club in his left. He pointed the gun at arm's length. 'Both of you stay still.'

Dates and Eves shared a glance, Dates slowly placing her arm behind her back as they stepped closer.

With his hands raised, Eves looked at Casey and smiled. 'What's going on, buddy. This is too weird even for you. You're scaring me.'

Casey gazed beyond him into the trees. 'I did what she asked. I brought her here. It's all she wanted all along.'

'You've done well,' Eves said. 'There's no need for the girl now. We can go home soon.'

Casey clenched his eyes shut. 'She speaks to me always. She's in my head night and day.'

Eves nodded. 'Hopefully, that'll soon be over.'

An expression of calm settled onto Casey's face. A look of compassion shone in his eyes as though all his demons had suddenly deserted him. He gave Eves the strangest smile, then, with the aim and swiftness of a man accustomed to such deeds, shot him in the head

As Eves's body dropped to the ground, Dates reached for her gun. The man-beast proved too quick, and the heavy thwack of wood against her face knocked her onto her back. Another smack followed. Pain surged through her body and kept her grounded, the sounds of the woods growing more distant as her thoughts and senses drifted to another place.

Gunshot filled the air, and Dates waited to breathe her last breath. But her heart kept beating, and as she tried opening her eyes, something heavy fell beside her, and the warm touch of human flesh brushed against her skin.

Among the blurred shafts of light, a thin pale figure gazed down at her. Dates lay motionless while it leant over her, feeling its lips press against her ear, inhaling its sour breath carried by each whisper. The voice told of things that only Dates could know, hauntings buried deep, stories of a neglected child, feelings of ugliness, men's cruel words–the perfect ingredients for a life plagued by disaster.

The voice promised to cure her ills, urging Dates to do its bidding, to eradicate the Quinby's of this world whose ego, greed and indulgences made them weak.

Years of repressed memories flooded Dates's mind. She tried hard to resist, recoiling at the touch of an uncle's wayward hands, glowering at a mother high on Valium. Anger raged inside her. Her hatred was directed at some older kid kicking her for no reason, at the boys in school telling her she was ugly, and at a pretty girl who once spat in her face.

What is the land without a queen to reign, it whispered, and *a worm to serve and turn the earth*?

Who was Dates to disagree? She reached for her gun, casting such memories from her mind, knowing some things were best left in the dark.

PART II

THE SPIDER AND THE FLY

1

What could Dates hope to achieve, battered and bruised, feeling as lifeless as the bodies scattered around her? She did what she needed to do, dig deep, and make the most of an ugly situation.

Even when dead, Casey was a brute. The big man must have weighed over two hundred and twenty pounds, and Dates needed to stop and catch her breath as she lugged his body behind a heap of fallen trees, a trail of blood snaking her through the grass. Eves was much lighter, although his contorted face was scarcely recognisable. There was no trace of the girl, and Dates searched for her through the woods.

Dates discovered the dead girl inside the abandoned watchtower. She lay slumped against the wall, her semi-naked body battered and grey, a trace of serenity lingering in her sunken eyes as though she had finally found peace. In better circumstances, Dates wouldn't have left her here; but time was at a premium, so she buried her as best she could.

Dates decided checking out of the White Hart pub was the best way to cover her tracks. Frank might grow suspicious otherwise, and the last thing she needed was the police stopping her as she headed south. When she arrived at the White Hart, Frank's face almost broke into a smile when Dates told him, 'We're leaving.'

He put down the glass he was polishing and studied her with a questioning eye. 'Where's Eves and Casey?'

'They went on ahead. I drew the short straw; they left the dirty work to me.'

'And what dirty work's that?'

'Check out, grab their stuff, put things right.'

'*Put things right*, in what way?'

'The only way we can, *financially*.'

Frank narrowed his eyes. 'Are you all right?'

'I'm fine. What makes you ask?'

'You're as white as a sheet for a start.' He pointed at the gash across her forehead. 'That looks nasty. There's blood all over you.'

'I'm fine, just tripped in the woods, that's all.'

'Must have been one hell of a fall, although it doesn't surprise me Eves let you come here in this state.' Frank frowned. 'I'm wondering whether I should call an ambulance?'

Dates pressed her fingers into her palms, feeling the moisture on her hands. 'Trust me, I'm fine.'

'But I better–'

'I'm fine, Frank. There's no need to do that.'

He responded with a defeated shrug, snatched his keys, and grumbled something as Dates followed him upstairs.

Casey's room was the first port of call. Frank tried warning her, but nothing could prepare Dates for the deranged man-beast's lair as Frank eased open the door. The room stank as though someone had just died in there and, before doing so, had smeared themselves in their own excrement A scratched figure of a naked woman marked the wardrobe. An unworldly-looking shape that even the most artless vandal would have been ashamed of. Rhyming couplets, scrawled in blood, covered the walls, and Dates wondered what riddles Lucifer would muster as he met Casey at Hell's gate.

Dates spied a shopping bag crammed with stained clothes and, pretending it was what she was after, grabbed it and said, 'This must be it.'

Frank didn't move. He stood in silence, his eyes roaming the walls. 'Jesus,' he kept saying in an astounded, pitiful voice. But for all his prayers, Dates knew the Messiah couldn't help him.

Dates reached into her pocket and grabbed five twenties. 'Sorry about the mess. I'd no idea.' She shoved them into Frank's hand. 'This ought to cover it.'

Frank took the cash without protest, remaining speechless while leading Dates into Eves's room. Eves had packed all his belongings into a brown duffle bag with a typed manuscript placed on top of it. Dates grabbed them and rushed downstairs, dropping onto her haunches as she missed the last step.

Frank helped her up. 'I said you weren't right, girl. You need to rest here for a while if you won't let me take you to the hospital.'

Dates staggered to the door. 'I'm fine, light on my feet, that's all.'

'Well, you don't look fine to me.'

'Honestly, I'm okay.'

Frank shook his head. 'No, I'm not convinced.'

'I'm fine,' she said through gritted teeth.

'You need patching up. A bite to eat wouldn't go amiss. I'm not letting you go until–'

Dates felt for her High-Power, but luckily, the expression

on her face seemed enough to cause him to back off. Frank escorted her to the bar. 'I'll be seeing you,' Dates said, wondering if he'd call the police when a wary nod was his sole reply.

2

Half an hour into her journey, Dates pulled into a layby and slipped on one of Eves's jumpers. She took the cleanest she could find, a mustard-coloured V-neck, which was less conspicuous than her bloodstained blouse. She got back onto the road, thoughts chasing through her head, holding her anxiety at bay with every sigh. Sadly, Quinby was her only hope. Undoubtedly, he would try to silence her with every threat. But for all his connections, she wouldn't take no for an answer. This time the body count wasn't her fault. Quinby owed her for this one.

The traffic meandered into one lane. It seemed everyone was trying to get out. A dying sun reddened the sky and bled into the distant water. The girl's voice lingered in Dates's mind, causing her to turn the radio to full blast to drown it out. As she drove, abstracted flashbacks helped her to retrace the madness. She shook her head in disbelief, knowing that, given enough time, Casey's and Eves's death would become the things of myth. But what took place in those woods was real, as was the voice whispering in her head, resonating through her flesh and bones, rooting itself within. She needed Quinby to make things right, shout her down for messing up, remind her that these voices were nothing but a hired gun's conscience, that all our devilry lies within.

THE TAINTED NIGHT air hung cold and damp over the city, and the faint rush of traffic, like the dimming lights, was a cruel deception. Dates learnt years ago that London only feigned sleep and wasn't duped by its temporary hush and starry moonlit sky. Dark things skulked among these alleyways and streets, more so since she returned. A sense of dread hung over her as she bathed. Something unseen brooded inside her. The same thing that had unlocked her deepest fears and thrown away the key.

Dates hadn't felt this bleak since she was a kid, and no amount of washing could scrub the dirt out. She slunk further into the bath and soaked her head beneath the water, peering up at the light as she held her breath. She could end it all now. But all life was programmed to survive. Even that young girl's whispers latched onto something.

Whatever this sickness was, Dates had caught it in those woods; she should have heeded Frank's good advice and stayed away from the place. It had its work cut out, whatever it was. Dates wasn't going down as easily as Casey; it should have chosen a more forgiving host.

Dates got out of the bath, relishing the cool air against her skin. She sighed deeply in the knowledge that Casey and Eves's incompetence had deprived her of her ticket back in. 'No,' she said to her reflection. None of this was her fault. But regardless of what took place, Quinby owed her for this one. She would pay him a call after midnight. Suicidal tendencies might get the upper hand, but Dates wasn't planning on dying without helping that young girl in the hospital.

3

Dates arrived at Quinby's house just after 1 a.m. The place stood in darkness, the blinded windows reflecting the glow of the streetlights. She had all a woman could ever need: knives, brass knuckles, her trusted High-Power, and enough bullets to take out a small army. She even had Eves's manuscript stuffed down the back of her trousers in case it gave some unexpected insurance. She broke in through the back, like only a cat with barely a few lives knows how.

The smell of fine dining hung in the air, and her stomach rumbled in protest. The kitchen looked immaculate. Neatly placed ceramic pots, jars, and steel pans gleamed among the refrigerator's eerie hum. She crept into the hall, contemplating whether to slip upstairs or investigate what lurked behind the half-opened door on her left. The faint sound of laughter solved her dilemma, and she pushed the door open a little wider, staring down at her shadow cast across a wedge of yellowish light.

All seemed quiet, the stilted silence of a forced hush. She stepped gingerly into the room, noticing the half-empty wineglass on the coffee table, a discarded magazine, and the fresh butt print on the sofa.

Sensing someone sneaking up on her was a talent that had graced her since childhood. It was hard to articulate. A skill, due to the shady circles she frequented, that had grown in refinement. Reacting to the warm brush of breath against her neck, Dates repeatedly rammed the back of her head into her assailant's face. She reached for the groin, crushing his lame exhibits of manhood. He let out a girl-like yelp, then tried slipping his arm around Dates's throat. Dates jacked her shoulders, tucked in her chin, then grasped his wrist, forcing his puny arm over her head and pushing her ear behind his elbow. It was a classic armbar. All it took was one step back, apply a little pressure, and the yelps turned into moans as she sent him crashing onto his back.

The not-so-pretty boy stared up at her. Blood poured from his nose. A yellow stain seeped through his white slacks. Dates shook her head and stared down at him. 'You should have been nicer to me when we first met. Some might call this Karma.'

When he neither moved nor spoke, Dates grabbed his shoulders and lifted him onto the sofa. He was mostly skin and bone. A poor deluded fool who had just received a lesson in the limits of his capabilities. He used the back of his hand to wipe his nose, then mumbled something about being unable to breathe.

'Try sitting up and holding your head back.'

He did as he was told and, like a scolded child, asked for a glass of water. Dates's motherly instincts overrode her better judgement. No need to kick a man when he's down. Only men like Quinby exploited every weakness.

When she returned with the glass of water, the young man was trying to clean himself up. It was a lacklustre affair, and it was a good job she wasn't feeling mean; a few more strikes would have finished him off.

She handed him the glass. 'What's your name?'

'Christopher. Chrissy.'

'Well, Chrissy, this happens when you creep up on people.'

He replied with a bitter laugh. 'You're the one who broke in.'

'True, but you shouldn't have confronted me.'

Dates crouched down in front of him, resting her hands on his knees. 'So, Chrissy, where's the master of the house?'

He hesitated for a second then a hint of something flashed in his eyes. 'He's. He's out.' That second pause was a second too long. There was a trace of unease in his voice. *Experientia docet*, and from Dates's experience, Chrissy had just gambled his life expectancy on a lie.

Her eyes met his. 'Out to where precisely?'

Chrissy shrugged. 'He never said.'

'Did he say anything? Like when he was coming back?'

'Quentin rarely tells me anything. He does as he pleases.'

'Sounds about right, seeing as this is his house, and you're just one of his floozies. A pretty ornament just hanging around. He'll drop you like a nasty habit in a few years. There's no point trying to do him any favours. Why should both of us end up broke?'

'What do you mean?'

'I'm here to collect. There's no reason you shouldn't benefit too?'

He considered the question, a hefty dose of treachery brewing in those icy blue eyes. Dates knew that people reacted three ways to the truth: they either plunged into denial or got nasty or took stock of their feelings and studied their options. Chrissy appeared to be considering the latter. He wasn't as dumb as he looked. There was a brain inside his pretty head.

'He's in bed,' Chrissy said, 'flaked out an hour ago.'

'And our little set-to didn't disturb him?'

Chrissy shook his head. 'We were partying hard. He took a lot of shit. There'll be no waking him until the morning.' He flashed Dates a mischievous smile, like a kid about to tell his secrets. 'I'll show you if you like?'

Dates followed him upstairs, not believing his story, tapping her Hi-Power for reassurance, knowing she was a magnet for misfortune.

Chrissy pointed at an open door, and Dates followed his gaze, her eyes resting on the shadows cast on the newly made bed. Something clanged downstairs, and Dates knocked Chrissy to the floor before chasing after it.

Quinby's distinctive smell of cologne tainted the air, as did the dark associations that accompanied it. The hurried sound of footsteps led Dates down the hall towards the end door, which opened out onto some lighted steps. She followed them down into what, on first impressions, she guessed was the basement. On closer inspection, Dates realised it was so much bigger than that. A house beneath a house with a long passageway of closed doors concealing Quinby's horrors and deepest secrets.

Dates edged across the tiled floor, pushing down on the door handles until she reached the large, arched door at the end of the passageway. A voice whispered inside her, a momentary distraction of riddles and rhymes. A man's muffled laughter held her silent, and her heart thumped inside her throat as she stepped closer.

Dates took out her gun. In moments like these, a girl needed protection. The door opened with a shove; the room's white leather sofa, the cream floor tiles, the white walls and ceramic ornaments were accentuated by the brightness of the light. This was minimalism to the extreme. A designer's chic blanket of white concealing the hell that lurked beneath. It was like walking through heaven's door, and who knew what dark angels awaited within.

As Dates's eyes adjusted to the light, the room grew more ordinary. It appeared to be a ground-floor flat. It had a living room, bedroom, and bathroom, all with matching interiors. The door of the room facing her was shut, and the voice that called to her from behind it was unmistakable. Even in times of duress, Quinby sounded condescending.

'You messed up, Dates. Don't come any closer if you know what's good for you.'

Dates responded with a slew of bullets. The sound rang in her ears. Not even the Devil would have endured that. She kicked open the door, a heap of questions hurtling through her mind; then, as swiftly as the dart that spiked her neck, the main entrance slammed shut behind her.

She ran at it, seized the handle, pulling it with all her might. The blasted thing wouldn't budge. She tried shooting out the lock, but the bullets just sank in. There must have been something behind it, another reinforced steel door by its sound. The mugginess in her head intensified, and a sudden weakness spread through her bones, turning her limbs into dead weights. Her body sagged to the floor, a voice imploring her to get up, but all she had left were tears of anger.

4

'*Will you walk into the parlour? Said the Spider to the Fly.*' Quinby's voice sounded victorious and smug. His incessant chatter was even less bearable than the whispers. Dates promised herself that once her strength returned, she would tear every speaker from these walls, find the source of that relentless tinny voice and rip his heart out. '*You walked right into that one, Dates,*' he said. '*I had this sound system specially made in Taiwan. Remarkable. Don't you think? Chrissy played his part so well. He's a promising actor. The things these artists do to kick start their careers. Although, I doubt little would surprise you.*'

A thickened tongue lolled inside her mouth, preventing her curses from bellowing out. She could barely sit up, couldn't even kick off the quilt covering her. A white hospital gown shrouded her aching body. The stiff cotton chaffed her skin, and through gritted teeth, she bore the torment of every itch. Consciousness fleeted in and out, each abstracted image blending into the next against the soundtrack of Quinby's rambling. '*It'll be some time until you feel right, Dates. There's lots of food in the kitchen should you regain your appetite. Read Eves's manuscript if your mind wanders. There's no reason you shouldn't know what's to become of you; try to cling to those small parts of yourself before it's too late.*

IF DATES WERE to die today, it wouldn't be in her own excrement. Never again would she underestimate the delight and satisfaction of being able to get herself to the restroom. Her dad had died in a hospital bed, a tube fixed to his dick, sores on his behind the size of bedpans. That kind of degradation was death's best accomplice. But Dates vowed nobody would be wiping her backside until her last breath.

How long had she been here? It was difficult to tell when the hours dragged like days. The lights turning on and off were a poor substitute for day and night. At least Quinby had the decency to stock up on alcohol. It amazed her how a few shots of whisky could drown out the whispers. But she was pacing herself. Alcohol preserved her sanity, but if she were to have any chance of surviving this, she needed to preserve her energy.

She felt vulnerable without her High-Power; her strength diminished like a fat man who had suddenly shed weight.

Each room merged into the next, white on white, the stifling air a lingering mix of cleaning products and newly laid carpet. Whenever Quinby spoke, the electricity cut out. The TV and the Hi-Fi were instantly muted, subservient to their master's voice.

Dates often screamed out Quinby's name, frequently asking him what the hell was going on? All he said was to calm herself, which she did, not because she heeded his advice but because she was a pro. Keeping it together is what she did. Survival never favoured the weak.

Staring at the speaker on the living room wall, Dates demanded her clothes.

'*You've no need for them,*' said Quinby's tinny voice. '*There are plenty of fresh gowns in the wardrobe.*'

Dates grabbed a fist full of hair, tempted to pull it out by the roots. 'Listen, Quinby, I did all you asked. It was Eves and Casey who screwed up. I was just a bystander, clearing up the mess as best I could. Don't project your grudges onto me. That young travelling girl is the victim here. Let's sit down and talk about it. You owe me.'

When he broke the long silence, a patronizing tone laced Quinby's voice. '*You shouldn't be too harsh on Eves and Casey; they played their parts perfectly. Admittedly, Eves's demise wasn't planned, but it worked to our advantage. And as for you, Dates, you've done everything I expected you to. Your willpower and predictability are second to none. You'll be the perfect host.*'

'Host?'

'*Are you acquainted with the waning moon? You've a few days before you lose yourself.*'

'You've lost me already. I'm sick of riddles. Stop playing your childish little games. What's all this about?'

Quinby sighed. '*I left you Eves's manuscript. Let's see if your brain is as smart as your mouth. I've even paid you the courtesy of retrieving your glasses; you'll find them in the top drawer of the bedside table. Read something for a change. See if you can work it out.*'

With so few options available to her, Dates took Quinby's advice. Eves's manuscript rested open on her lap, her glass of vintage malt glinting beneath the lamplight. Information was power, so she'd been told and kept that in mind as she began reading *The Strange Lives of Helenora Haye*.

PART III

THE STRANGE LIVES OF HELENORA HAYE

BY DR SEBASTIAN EVES (DRAFT 1)

1

The Flintshire lowlands in the northeast corner of Wales have never sat easily with notions of Welsh identity. Before the 1536 Act of Union, the region had always been a curious amalgam of social and cultural contrasts. This in-between place, lying on the border between England and Wales, with easy access to the Dee estuary and English seaports, had always seen a steady flow of migrant workers.

By the time Helenora Haye was born in 1659, English was the established language of both business and commerce. The Flintshire lowlands, particularly the town of Holywell, were viewed with deep suspicion by many Welsh-speaking parts of Wales.

The local parish register shows that Helenora Sadler, only daughter of Jacob and Grace Sadler, was baptised at St James Church, Holywell, on June 28th, 1659. Newly born children were typically baptised a week following their birth or if mother and child were strong enough on the nearest Sunday. Helenora Sadler's birthday would have been on or around the summer solstice. This date would prove to be more significant in the centuries to come.

Little is known about Helenora's parents. Her father, originally from Shrewsbury, had settled in the area after the Civil War. There is no record of his former occupation, but between 1655-59, he gained land where he farmed wheat and barley until his death sixteen years later. Jacob Sadler was industrious and hardworking, climbing up the social ladder from labourer to husbandman, leaving an inheritance of £70 and land exceeding thirty acres.

Farm life was hard and primarily self-sufficient. From an early age, Helenora would have helped her mother cook, bake bread, brew beer, cure bacon, salt meats, make pickles and preserves, and spin linen and wool. Helenora's mother also taught her knowledge of medicines and healing, skills that Helenora would later pass on to her own daughter. Orthodox medical practitioners were rare and solely for the wealthy. Common people relied on magical healers, cunning folk and charmers, practices that carried a tremendous risk. If they failed to cure, they often resulted in accusations of witchcraft.

Helenora's mother was exceptional because she had received, albeit informally, an education. Literacy was solely for the privileged, and Helenora, as future testimony shows, was schooled by her mother in reading and writing, a rare gift for a husbandman's daughter. Literate and skilled in the arts of magical healing, both mother and daughter would undoubtedly have been regarded with an air of fear and suspicion. Misgivings festered and had grave consequences for Helenora in the years following her mother's death.

Parish records show that Grace Sadler died from dysentery in the winter of 1672. In the spring of 1673, Helenora was married to farm labourer Simond Haye, and their daughter Eme was born ten months later. Initially, Simond Haye did well from his father-in-law's smallholding; as a dowry, he was given land and inherited all thirty acres on Jacob Sadler's death.

On the surface, he appears to have managed the lands well; however, local court records documenting his fines for breach of the peace and time spent in the pillory tell another story. Witness testimonies confirm that Simond Haye spent most of his time in alehouses. It is logical to conclude that Helenora managed the land and the household, skills and responsibilities she had learnt from early childhood. Yet, for all Simond Haye's shortcomings, he must have been fond of his wife. After his sudden and unexpected death in 1678, Helenora inherited the entire estate, providing her with a secured widowhood.

It was during the early years of widowhood that Helenora's troubles began. After her husband's death, his sister, Barbary Craggs, claimed her brother's land, arguing that it had been promised her shortly before his death. Naturally, the claim was refuted, and a vicious feud followed, resulting in Craggs accusing Helenora of devil worship to empower her, which resulted in the murder, by an incurable illness, of Simond Haye.

In the 17th century, belief in witchcraft was ubiquitous. From remote villages to large cities, witchcraft affected people's everyday lives, in various forms, across Europe and North America, with, as in Helenora Haye's case, hostilities between families and neighbours encouraging suspicion and accusations. One commonly held belief was in the supernatural abilities of witches. It was believed that having copulated with the devil or one of his many demons, the witch had the power to damage crops, kill livestock, cause sexual impotence, frigidity, bareness, and, as illustrated in the accusations made against Helenora Haye, inflict incurable illnesses.

Barbary Craggs claims to have witnessed Helenora converse with a tall, broad man with a serpent's tail in Heron Copse near the small upland village of Ysceifiog. The village name translates as "a place where elder trees grow." As a secluded spot with splendid views, it became a favourite haunt for Helenora and her young daughter.

There are few legal records of the case; however, it appears from the brief entries by town clerk John Jones that it did not go to trial. Helenora's education would have aided her with this outcome. Having inherited the money that she had persuaded her late husband to set up for her as a trust, she was in a good position, unlike many widows, to win favour and buy people's silence. However, Helenora's good fortune would not last, and her trial that would take place a few years later would have disastrous consequences.

It started with her friendship and, as later accusers would testify, sexual relationship with yeoman Oswald Rand. Although far from the privileged ranks of a squire, with over two hundred acres, Rand was renowned throughout the area and carried a modicum of influence. Rand attained his wealth through his marriage to Malda Stott. She was a sickly, often bedbound woman, making their relationship far from harmonious alongside Rand's constant philandering.

Rand's confession states that he first sought Helenora's services in the spring of 1683. It was a time before divorce with no legal way to dissolve a valid marriage. The only way to break the union was to prove that the marriage had never been lawful. For most, this was not an option; they were fated to endure a life of misery until their own or, if they were fortunate enough, their spouse's death. However, Rand's carnal lust for a woman twenty years his junior placed him in a position where he could no longer bear the agonising wait.

After two days of intensive torture, Rand confessed, telling his interrogators it was Helenora Haye who had initially approached him. Troubled by her ex-lover's state of mind and concerned for his welfare, Haye, having confessed to Rand that she had practised witchcraft for years, gifted him with a grey powder, instructing him to place it in a tart of boiled milk and feed it to his wife. With no other way out, Rand did as he was told, returning to Haye three days later when the supernatural poison proved unsuccessful. Rand returned to his home with a more lethal dose; however, unbeknown to him, his wife, having suffered from a mysterious illness, grew suspicious and confided to close friends that she feared her husband was trying to poison her.

On April 4th, 1683, they found Malda Rand dead in her bed, having complained of "sticking and prickling" pains the previous evening. Even before Malda's burial, rumours about the suspicious circumstances of her death ran rife throughout the neighbourhood. Other stories quickly followed.

One told of how a tall, broad demonic figure, who, they later claimed, was in league with Helenora Haye, entered Malda Rand's room by transforming into a crow and pecking at her skin. Another rumour told of how Helenora Haye, seen as quarrelsome and an outsider by many people within the community, had argued and subsequently fallen out with farm labourer Nycholas Tayler, a close friend of Barbary Craggs.

Tayler claimed the dispute began after scolding Helenora's daughter, Eme, for teasing local simpleton Mary Cowper and trespassing on her parents' land. Young Eme strongly contested this, insisting that she and Mary were close friends and were playing a game that Tayler had deliberately misconstrued. Eme ran to her mother, and according to Tayler, a furious Helenora threatened him with revenge, muttering strange words as she cursed him. Tayler thought little of it, mocking Helenora as he recalled the argument to his cronies in the local alehouse.

It was not until a few days later that Tayler took the threats more seriously. One morning whilst working the fields, Taylor caught sight of a black dog staring at him from the lane opposite. He describes it as "large like a wolf" with "red eyes that were fierce and gut-foundered." The dog watched him for a while, causing the plough horse and the cows in the adjacent field to grow restless, especially when the animal started spinning in circles. Tayler tried scaring the dog away, but with every attempt, it grew fiercer. The dog watched him until the end of Tayler's working day and followed him to his house. Tayler did not attend the alehouse that night. He retired to his bed early, his body riddled with aches and pains, and before dawn, he was drenched in sweat and shivering with a high fever.

Tayler claims Helenora visited him that day, offering to remove the curse, providing he apologised to young Eme, and having satisfied herself that Tayler was ready to do so, she gave him a parchment of grey powder, instructing him to place it in a flagon of ale and, once recovered that he was to take this as a final warning.

Other rumours ensued, with Oswald Rand confessing to Helenora Haye's involvement in his wife's death in the days following his arrest. On April 12th, 1683, Helenora Haye was arrested and placed in Ruthin Gaol. At first, Helenora was questioned without torture; however, when she refused to confess, she was subjected to three more days of interrogation. Thumbscrews were a standard instrument of the times, and those unfortunate to experience such agony would readily admit to anything.

There are no existing records of Helenora Haye's interrogation. Although based on similar trials and witch-hunts, there is little doubt that she must have suffered considerably. She would have been stripped and examined for the devil's mark. Starved, exhausted, and suffering from excruciating pain on April 16th, 1683, Helenora Haye confessed to the following charges:

Carnal Copulating with the devil
 For witchcraft and murder of Simond Haye
 For witchcraft and murder of Malda Rand
 Bewitchment of Oswald Rand
 Bewitchment of Nycholas Tayler
 Consulting with evil spirits in the form of a familiar.

On April 26th, 1683, Helenora Haye was arraigned and executed by hanging. Her story reflects the fate of many others who suffered from the witch hysteria of the seventeenth century. A victim of circumstance, many would argue. A young woman whose suggested sexual promiscuity did not sit comfortably with the puritanical mindset of the age. An outspoken widow, a troublesome outsider, a woman whose frequent bickering with her neighbours would sow the seeds of the malevolence. However, centuries after Helenora Haye's death, a letter surfaced, deemed authentic, which sheds new and more sinister light on her story.

The letter in mention was written by

Helenora Haye during her time at Ruthin Gaol and smuggled out to her daughter Eme, assumedly by a jailor. The letter reads thus:

"Dearly beloved Eme, *it is with crippled hands I write, and blood runs from my fingernails. Though my body is pained and battered beyond its years, I would endure these tortures tenfold to have this letter be with you. For you are my rock. You are the solitary yellow flame in this world of darkness. Unrepentant, I come into gaol. Unrepentant have I been under torture. Unrepentant, I must die. Keep faith in me, dear daughter. Obey all my wishes, and our bond will travel beyond death. And once again, we will be reunited. But should this not come to pass. Then know that my confession to them is only part of the story. And I disclose such secrets to you so you may know all of it.*

My persecutors proclaimed that a woman's weakness is carnal lust. Dearest daughter, you are too young to understand their words. But know this: the many desires of men lead to all sins. My father was a pious, god-fearing man. But behind the mask was a brute creation. My mother kept me safe from him. For his eyes never fixed on his wife but often wandered across the body of his own daughter. It made me abjure his beliefs, forsake the holy Christian faith, and swear loyalty to the old ways.

Now, dear child, I love you as deeply as my mother loved me, and I have taught and versed you in the ways of the Cunning folk just as my mother had taught me. But thanks to my mother's schooling, I was blessed with greater fortune. When I was little older than yourself, I often played in Heron Copse, idling among the trees. It was there that I first met Bathin, great Duke of hell, commander of thirty legions. He was strong and broad, riding a pale horse, his serpent tail slithering over the beast's flesh. He praised how I had denounced God and promised me power and life beyond my years if I adored forever to him and the devil. I was deeply troubled at first until Bathin begged me not to be anxious. Then I yielded to his will. And after letting him guide me onto my knees, I kissed his posterior and attached a black candle to his tail, announcing my love and servitude, entreating that he guide me to crush my enemies, be they beast, woman, or man.

Dear daughter, I served Bathin well, travelled with him at night, and attended his nocturnal dances. And when asked to show the strength of my allegiance, I could not bring myself to sacrifice my beloved daughter, and when Bathin saw my sad plight, accepted my offering of your father.

Now, dearest child, know that I was deeply troubled by this. And know that your father was a swill-belly like his father before him. A mulligrubs and idle borachio who was only chirping-merry when he was wasting our hard-earned coin in the alehouse. He neglected my father's land, and we would have grown destitute if left to the mercy of his vices. And my Duke's recompense benefited us both, as did his guidance that I should inherit what was my birthright.

Now, my child, learn this and learn it well. Folk are weak, and though there is kindness in this world, there is more hate and jealousy. Malice that you are only spared if folk fear you. Folk are good when they can take what they need, but when denied their fill, the godly are quick to turn against you. I have known this all my life and have not always taken heed of such wisdom. Malice is the enemy of complacency. My fate, dearest Eme, is a testament to that, as is the spite of that wicked pickthank Barbary Craggs.

Now, know this dearest child; weakness in others is also your enemy. I have learned this at my cost. Folk should know not to betray you for fear of the vilest reprisal. The sins and folly of weak men also harm you as my fate attests from the treachery of that beard-splitter Rand. My wish is that I may speak these words to you. Do not fear, dearest daughter, though, by the time you read this letter, I am hung by the neck and my naked body cast into a crevice with the rats. We will be reunited. Do as I bid you.

Take the fourth parchment from my hiding place and guide Mary Cowper to Heron Copse. Summon the great Duke as I have shown you, and once poor Mary has willingly read the parchment aloud, the great Bathin himself will guide you. For he knows the virtues of herbs and precious stones and makes the spirits of men and women possess the body of others. And afterwards and forevermore, I will be with you.

Dearest Eme, this letter must remain secret. For those who have persecuted and tortured me will do the same unto you. And the thought of your suffering saddens me more than my own plight.

Be strong, dearest daughter, for we will see each other beyond this darkness that lesser men believe to be light.

Helenora Haye April 1683"

2

Assuming the letter's authenticity, it allows us to draw several conclusions. First, these are the delusions of a troubled woman. A paranoid schizophrenic whose tenuous grasp of reality became pushed beyond breaking point by the horrors of intense interrogation and extreme torture. Exhausted and suffering agonising pain, Helenora Haye, like so many victims who endured the same fate, was driven to believe the diabolical claims of her accusers. A mother whose love for her daughter allowed her to proclaim the ability to return after death, to provide comfort to the child and as a last desperate attempt to offer hope.

An opposing argument might be that everything Helenora Haye confessed to her daughter was true. That she, as her mother before her, practised witchcraft and to acknowledge her loyalty, the great Duke

Bathin would reward her. Therefore, continuing with this premise, the obvious question is: What proof do we have of this?

There are few written records concerning what happened to Eme Haye after her mother's execution. However, the witchcraft pamphlet account of Helenora Haye's trial refers to Eme Haye's and Mary Cowper's disappearance shortly after Helenora's death. In the centuries to follow, local gossip and superstition would turn the story of the girls' sudden absence into local myth. The legend tells how Eme Haye lured Mary Cowper to Heron Copse, later referred to locally as Witches Copse. It was there that the spirit of Helenora Haye possessed the poor simple girl, cursing the village before leaving with her daughter to do the devil's bidding and returning to the copse every seven years to give sacrifice beneath the witch's new moon.

Today, Witches Copse lies lost among a larger wood. However, its original spot is marked by a ruinous tower, rumoured to be a Roman Pharos. However, records show they built it in 1887 to mark Queen Victoria's Golden Jubilee. Even in these modern times, the place, with its thick cluster of eerie high trees, and its twisted shadows in the half-light, lies steeped in an atmosphere of foreboding. Some claim that on winter nights beneath the glow of a witch's moon, the possessed can hear Helenora Haye softly calling. Like many stories in Wales, the legend of Helenora Haye has all the familiar folklore tropes. Yet it is unique because, unlike other tales, Helenora's story does not fade into obscurity, destined to be a brief paragraph in a folk-tale anthology.

In 1884, two hundred years after Helenora Haye's death, office clerk Walter Parry from Carshalton in the London Borough of Sutton appeared before the magistrates' court charged with threatening behaviour against his wife, Ida. On the surface, this was a standard domestic abuse case. However, closer inspection sheds it in a more curious and sinister light.

Walter Parry was a law-abiding citizen. Parry was an unlikely candidate for such aggressive behaviour, a regular churchgoer with a good position. As part of his defence, Parry claims that the person he attacked was not his wife but the foreign spirit that had possessed her. His testimony shows that the couple were happily married before his wife's "illness." Ida had been a model wife, taking good care of the house and a loving mother to their two children. Her troubles began following a short family holiday at Bognor Regis. The holiday was a great success. Both husband and wife felt revived, especially Ida, who had taken early morning walks along the coast. Walter Parry noticed a slight change in his wife's personality on returning home. Ida, who was talkative by nature, was quieter than usual. She seemed sullen, seen mumbling to herself, and often appeared distracted. At first, Parry put his wife's strange behaviour down to tiredness. However, Parry's worry increased when the symptoms persisted, aggravated by a series of bad dreams.

As the nightmares continued, Ida often awoke exhausted, bedbound for days, tearful and delirious, and her protestations becoming more incomprehensible. Walter tried various concoctions from the local apothecary, and when Ida showed no progress, he resorted to bleeding by leeches. Every attempt to restore Ida back to good health proved futile. They summoned the doctor, who recommended a "change of air," diagnosing Ida with a mild case of neurasthenia.

After heeding the doctor's advice, Ida Parry made excellent progress following a short convalescence. The nightmares stopped, her energy levels returned, and she became more coherent. However, despite the positive news, Walter Parry remained adamant that Ida was not the woman she was. As he explained to the magistrates, "my wife was still lost to me."

Walter remained adamant the spirit of a woman called Helenora Haye possessed Ida. "There's this look about her," he told the court, "Cold and clever. My Ida was a kind soul, but this woman never smiles, and whenever I catch her staring at me, her eyes are absent of all feeling."

When asked how Ida was with the children, Walter replied, "decent enough, I suppose, but a lot stricter than she ever was, but the thing that hurts me most was that whenever they called her mother, she scolded them and insisted they refer to her as Ms Haye."

As Ida's personality grew more unrecognisable, Walter also had nightmares. He faced a difficult dilemma: either try to cope with the recent upheavals or inform the authorities of Ida's possession, which risked them both being committed to an asylum. After confiding his troubles to close friends, one of them pointed him to an elderly widow known as Ma Morgan. The old woman dealt in herbs and home remedies, a clairvoyant and back-alley abortionist. If she had been born two hundred years earlier, she would have suffered the same fate as Helenora Haye.

Walter Parry was reluctant at first, but after some persuasion and having no other options, the fretful husband contacted the old widow and related the story of his wife. Parry describes Ma Morgan as a "troubling sight;" he comments on her "furrowed skin," her "white straggly hair," and her "unnerving toothless grin." Yet he quickly revised his initial opinion, realising that she was a "woman of great knowledge and understanding." It was easy to understand why "people warmed to her."

Ma Morgan listened in silence and, after a brief deliberation, agreed with Walter Parry that his wife was possessed, although not by an aimless demonic spirit. Instead, she claimed Ida Parry's recent ailments were because of witchcraft. Parry would have laughed at such notions if presented with this idea several months ago. However, having endured months of domestic turmoil, he accepted it and grew eager to heed Ma Morgan's advice.

The old woman instructed him to break the spell and act fast before completely losing his wife. Ma Morgan advised him to blood the witch. Those who had been afflicted typically "scratched a witch." However, as Parry's wife was both the possessor and the possessed, Ida needed to draw blood. Ma Morgan insisted that it was necessary to be above the neck for the "blooding" to be effective. However, in extreme cases where the afflicted had succumbed to the witch's spirit, decapitation was the only form of release.

On Saturday, September 6th, 1884, Walter Parry followed his wife while taking her daily morning walk. Ma Morgan had advised him to act quick. Still, Parry, eager to end it, explained to the magistrates that he could not allow his children to witness the "blooding" and had to choose the right moment.

Parry confronted his wife in Carshalton Park. Key witnesses and the couple who intervened, Alice and Samuel Verlow, told the magistrates how Parry chased after his wife as though he were a "madman." The couple described the attack as "inhumane," relating how Parry "dragged" his wife "by the hair" before "slicing her head with a penknife." When Ida retaliated, he knocked her onto the ground, fell onto his knees and wept, begging for her forgiveness.

It was a strange case; however, with Walter Parry being a man of moral character until this trial and Ida Parry corroborating every part of her husband's testimony, the magistrates felt obliged to show leniency.

Perhaps Ida Parry's symptoms were psychosomatic, and her husband, pushed beyond his tether, was desperate enough to believe anything. However, even if this was the case, it still does not explain how Ida Parry became aware of Helenora Haye? The chronology of these troubling events seems to point to the couple's initial holiday as the starting point. Who knows what the catalyst might have been? Yet recent, similarly frightening events might shed light on this.

3

July 1978 saw cooler weather than previous summers, an omen for the harsh winter and the cold climate that presently engulfs us. As the cooler air settled beneath grey skies, larger than average rainfalls spoiled day trips and family holidays. Determined to sit out the foul weather, the Moran family, originally from Liscarroll, set up camp on the outskirts of Amesbury, a small town near Salisbury Plain. As with most traveller sites, the new visitors did not sit well with the local inhabitants. However, there were no significant incidents except for a few police call-outs, and the Morans managed to keep a low profile.

The Morans made their living by breaking down cars and selling parts, building a mess of scrap metal and clutter around them. It was common to see the younger children running wild, playing on swings, or sitting around one of its many campfires. They had little to no education. The family left it to their sixteen-year-old daughter, Hetty, to provide basic schooling.

Hetty was a bright and artistic girl. Extrovert and articulate, she was often the key person when dealing with official notices and administration. As a natural, free spirit, Hetty spent hours roaming the plains, wandering among the white chalk downs and the outskirts of Stonehenge. The family, especially the small children, often teased that she was a witch. She was an avid reader of the 'occult' and all things 'supernatural.'

Friday 21st July 1978 was a typical working day for the Morans. The men were out scouring the area for scrap metal; the women tended to the campfires and the caravans while the children ran wild, playing on the burgeoning pile of debris. Hetty had gone for a walk. She would be out for hours, returning on or around midday, so the family remained unconcerned when she had not returned by late afternoon.

By 7 p.m. that evening, the worry kicked in. Jack Moran and his two elder sons, Danny and Sean, took to their van and searched for Hetty, driving through the narrow country lanes and questioning every passer-by. At 9 p.m., there was still no sign of her. Suspicious of the authorities and reluctant to call the police, Jack ventured into the town. Travelling families were often barred from the local pubs, and visiting these establishments came with significant personal risk. Animosities ran high, and if anyone had seen Hetty, they were certainly keeping it to themselves. With most of his options exhausted, Jack Moran went back to the site, collected his dogs, and formed a small search party.

It was cloudy that night and difficult to cover much ground, aided only by flash lamps and torchlight. They kept calling Hetty's name, their shouts growing more frantic, as did the dogs' relentless barking. A low mist was rising, and as midnight drew closer, Jack Moran was ready to give up and resume his search in the morning. As Jack and his boys headed back to the van, Jack's trusted lurcher, Max, caught the scent of something. The dog bolted up the hill, sprinting towards a copse of trees. Jack and his boys gave chase, exchanging worried glances when Max abruptly came to a stop, rested on its stomach, and started whining.

Now only a few yards away, it was not Max's distress that troubled the Morans but the shivering semi-naked Hetty huddled before them. Dressed in nothing but her underwear, the girl was pale and distraught. As Jack covered her with his coat and lifted her into his arms, he dreaded to think about what might have happened to her. The boys tried quizzing her during the drive home. Although gentle in their approach, Hetty was delirious, mumbling to herself, and they could not get any sense from her.

When the party arrived back at the site, the women took charge, bathing the poor girl and quickly getting her to bed. Few rested on the site that night. The Morans discussed what had happened until the early hours of the morning. The boys demanded retribution. However, Jack insisted they would do nothing until they got to the truth of it. All they could do was wait. At least Hetty was sleeping now, her breathing more settled, the family thankful that the girl did not have a fever.

In the days that followed, Jack and his boys kept asking around the town. An altercation took place between Sean and one of the locals. As expected, the Morans took the blame, which resulted in the campsite being visited by the police. Jack let it slip about Hetty during the ensuing argument, and a woman constable accompanied Hetty during a police interview. Hetty was still in no fit state to be questioned, let alone by the authorities. The exercise proved pointless, and Jack, pushed beyond patience, received a police caution after voicing his frustrations.

Jack was in a quandary. The local inhabitants, supported by the authorities, urged the family to move on. The Morans often ignored such threats. Yet, with his daughter showing signs of decline, Jack became eager for a change of scenery. The family fell into dispute. Some wanted to stay put and wait until Hetty could shed more light on the incident, while others agreed it would benefit the girl to get away. It was a family divided; however, Hetty herself would force the family to decide.

After everything she had been through, the Morans willingly tolerated the changes in Hetty's personality: the faraway look in her eyes, the quiet detachment, the regular bout of frightening nightmares. Jack, who often sought solace in a bottle of whisky, proclaimed his daughter was lost to him. There was talk of getting her help and signing her into a mental hospital. Every discussion concerning Hetty ended in a row. However, none of these quarrels compared to the argument on Thursday, August 3rd, 1978, when Hetty, washed and dressed in her best clothes, announced she was leaving the site.

When Jack told her to stay, she declared that "no man nor woman was her master." Her personality, just like Ida Parry a hundred years before her, shifted between the poor confused girl they found that night on the fields and the irrepressible, confident Helenora Haye.

They summoned the local priest. The children watched from the bonfires, unsure whether to laugh or cry as Hetty screamed her protests from the confines of Jack's caravan. It had just turned midday when the nervous, reluctant Father Hamilton arrived at the site. With a bible held firmly in his hand, he let the Morans escort him along the muddy makeshift path. Witnesses claim that Jack told Father Hamilton that his daughter was "lost" and "confused." However, when the local papers printed the story, they claimed that Jack Moran believed his daughter was "bewitched."

Regardless of the words used, Jack Moran had grown desperate. Irreligious by nature, Jack demanded that Father Hamilton perform an exorcism. The priest refused. Hetty needed a medical examination first. Even if found to be of sound mind, they still required the bishop's approval. The Morans offered him money. Jack even swore to change his heathen ways and pray for God's forgiveness.

The young priest stood his ground, explaining that the best he could do was speak with her. With limited options, the Morans accepted, with Father Hamilton offering to guide the girl through confession too. The young priest's good intentions exceeded his experience, and nothing could prepare him for the backlash. Jack told Father Hamilton to stay back. Then he warned Hetty they were coming in. An eerie silence fell over the camp as Jack unlocked the door. A wedge of sunlight cut through the dark, exposing the serene image of Hetty standing before them.

Father Hamilton told her not to be frightened. Yet the tremor in his voice betrayed his veneer of bravado. He stepped inside, and Hetty attacked him when she caught sight of his bible. When later questioned by a local reporter, the shaken young priest stated that the assault was so ferocious and blasphemous that it shall be "forever ingrained upon his memory."

Worried about the girl's safety, the family agreed Hetty needed to leave. Travelling as a group would slow them down, so Jack insisted he should go with her alone. No one protested, and when asked where he would take her, a distraught and defeated Jack replied, "to north Wales, those woods she keeps talking about."

A group of truant schoolboys reported the first sighting of Hetty Moran at Witches Copse. No one knew where she came from or how she got there. Rumour had it that the abandoned white van, a few miles from the woods, had something to do with it. Such a frightening sight, seeing her that dull September morning. Initially, the boys thought she was a ghost because of Hetty's deathly paleness. Her waist-length, matted hair hung stiffly against her dirty skin. Torn clothes, exposed cuts and bruises, and her green eyes, sunken into a gaunt face, penetrated your whole being.

News of the girl travelled fast. Many

believed it to be a hoax, mischievous constructs of a schoolboy's imagination. Those less cynical tried investigating the matter further. They notified the police, but there was little they could do with no actual crime committed, and they failed to take it seriously. Opinion remained divided. The sceptics grew concerned for a troubled girl who had sadly lost her way. Whereas the superstitious were wary of the spirit that possessed her and the legend of Helenora Haye. Yet if there was one thing on which both parties could agree, it was not to venture to *Witches Copse* beyond midnight.

As we near the latter half of the twentieth century, belief in the supernatural remains widespread. Regardless of all our advances in medicine and science, folklore and superstition prevail, particularly in remote rural villages. Legends such as Helenora Haye's are not unique. Yet few stories are as durable. A mythology that refuses to disappear. A fascinating tale that grows more worthy of investigation.

Although separated by more than a century, the lives of Ida Parry and Hetty Moran share a common bond. The similarity between the women's fate is more than mere coincidence. Delve deeper into their story, and you unlock its mystery. A secret, under the right conditions, which is easily replicated.

Aided by my research partner Jack Casey,

I arrived at the tiny village of Ysceifiog on a bleak January 2nd in the early evening. We booked ourselves into the local, and only, pub. The disgruntled landlord gave us an equally cold welcome. From what I gathered, we were the only residents. So, I paid him a month in advance to dissuade him from asking too many questions. It did the trick. Mostly he left us alone. But I noticed the nervous look on his face when I mentioned we would work up at Witches Copse. When asked what he knew about the travelling girl, the landlord was reluctant to talk about it. "Nothing," he told me with a shrug. Yet his forced nonchalance failed to hide the worry on his face. An expression that became graver when he warned me to "stay away from those woods."

When I asked him why, he declined to answer, remaining silent no matter how much I prompted him. I grew more thankful for the landlord's distance as the days passed. Long dreary days spent in the damp solitariness of those woods took their toll, more so on Jack Casey. We saw little of Hetty Moran. Rare glimpses of her pale, emaciated face haunted us among the trees. Her voice travelled along with the wind, growing feebler every time we heard it. Just as Ida Parry had struggled a hundred years before, Hetty Moran's mind, body and soul proved too fragile. To weaken the link, Casey would serve as an initial carrier. Yet it soon became clear we needed a stronger host.

I first met Elizabeth May Daton, or Dates as she preferred to call herself, in the White Hart pub on a dismal January evening. A mercenary by trade, the project's sponsor chose Dates after careful consideration. Not only did her unique talents catch our attention, but also the similarities she shared with Ida Parry, Hetty Moran and Helenora Haye.

Research shows that all four women were born on or around the summer solstice. This bears great significance, as some ancient mystic texts decree children born during this time are magical, with a natural ability for spirit possession, either acting as a vessel or enabling their own spirit to pass from one body to the next. Arguably, it is an interesting premise. However, evidence shows that

PART IV

THE ORDER OF THE CRESCENT MOON

1

Dates hurled Eves's manuscript at the door, watching a shower of paper sheets fall across the carpet. She glared at the lopsided speaker on the wall, and although the dreams and the voices in her head told her otherwise, she yelled, 'You're insane, Quinby. Do you actually believe all this?'

The lack of response emphasised the room's silence. Dates high-kicked the speaker off the wall. 'That poor girl had barely turned sixteen, hadn't even lived a quarter of her life for Chrissake.'

A low crackling sound preceded the tinny voice. '*Two other people lost their lives; one was a close friend of mine.*'

Dates momentarily closed her eyes and sighed. 'To hell with them. They took their chances. Poor Hetty was innocent. Eves and Casey got what they deserved, interfering with people's heads, long overdue if you ask me.'

'*Nobody did,*' came Quinby's curt reply. '*What did you think of Eves's manuscript? A tad ornate in parts but quite illuminating, I think. It's a shame he never got to finish it.*'

Dates suppressed the scream by closing her eyes, the warm air forcing her to swallow against the dryness in her throat. She scowled at the smell of boil-in-the-bag dinners and new carpet, a sickening mix that had badgered her for days now. She opened her eyes and, in her calmest voice, said, 'It's a lot to take in, Quinby. Any chance we can discuss this face to face? Outside even? I've been cooped up for ages. Let me have some fresh air, at least.'

The dismounted speaker crackled back to life. '*Let me see what can be arranged. I'll get back to you.*' Quinby chuckled. '*In the meantime, stay put.*'

DATES SQUINTED into the lighted corridor like a startled rat suddenly freed from its cage. It had shrunk since she last saw it, and a steel wall sealed off two-thirds. Only a short hallway remained, leading to an open door. Dates crept along the wood-tiled floor and stepped into a wedge of light.

It seemed like years since she'd been outside, and blinded by the winter sun, she relished the cool air across her face. Once her eyes adjusted to the daylight, she took in the surrounding courtyard divided by a high wall made from thick tempered glass.

Among the distance rush of traffic, she noted the exit to the road. Unfortunately, she was on the wrong side–the story of her life these days. She felt both reassured and saddened that the city had continued without her. Happy at being another insignificant speck on the landscape, she preferred the company of strangers. She'd long ago resigned herself to a life among the shadows, but she refused to die in this place.

The entourage who stood opposite her seemed excessive even by Quinby's standards. But it was the man to her captor's right that caught her attention. Standing over six-foot-tall, the furrowed brow made his dark eyes more menacing. The greying slicked-back hair emphasised the strong cheekbones and square jawline. Except for the crow's feet around the eyes, the pallid complexion revealed little signs of ageing. A black three-piece velvet suit emphasised his tall, slender figure. Handsome by most tastes, Dates instantly despised him. She tried staring him down but quickly averted her gaze; his piercing stare remained unrelenting.

'Are you positive she's suitable,' he said from behind the glass, 'seems a trifle weak-willed to me.'

Quinby laughed. 'Don't let her looks fool you. There's a barrier between us for a good reason.'

'There's no need to worry, Dr Mannix,' said the raincoated henchman standing behind them. 'I've got this skank bitch in my sights. Even if that barrier wasn't there, I'd drop her at the slightest twitch.'

Dates didn't respond. The tall guy now had a name thanks to this loud-mouthed Neanderthal. Mannix cast Quinby a dismissive glance, who gave the henchman a look that said, 'keep your mouth shut.'

Dates studied the glass wall. Even if she scaled it, they would splatter her brains across the courtyard long before reaching the exit. She felt Quinby's eyes upon her, undecided what angered her more: the lies and deceit that had brought her here or the amused look on his face.

'Enjoying the fresh air, Dates?' Quinby said. 'Or is this inclement weather not to your tastes?'

Dates shrugged. 'The cold never bothers me. The smell of bullshit in the air angers me most.'

Once again, Quinby flashed her that ingratiating, self-satisfied smile. 'A tad unfair, don't you think? We've been transparent throughout. I instructed Eves to be honest with you. Tell people the truth, and they'll never spot the lie. I've been over-generous with my hospitality. Some might say the perfect host. I gave you Eves's manuscript, did I not? I'm even talking to you face to face as you requested.'

Dates shook her head in distaste. 'A ten-foot glass barrier between us is hardly face to face. I imagined a more intimate rendezvous; I wasn't expecting Dr Goebbels and his two stormtroopers here.'

Quinby attempted to say something but closed his mouth as Mannix held out his hand and silenced him with an authoritative 'shush.' Dates couldn't decide what impressed her more: Dr Mannix's self-assured demeanour or the way it slapped a disgruntled look across Quinby's face. Treating Quinby in such an off-handed manner was a sight few had witnessed, worsened by Quinby allowing Mannix to get away with it. A clear demonstration of power, a pecking order that Dates had only just grown aware of.

'You've a lot to say for yourself,' Mannix said. 'It surprises me you've lasted this long.'

Once again, Quinby tried to interject, but Mannix silenced him with a look. 'Please, Quentin, don't make me ask you again.'

Dates grinned. 'Yeah, do as you're told, *Quentin;* let the big boss deal with this.'

Quinby, glaring at her red-faced, fell silent.

Mannix studied her with a disapproving eye. 'So, this is the much talked about Elizabeth May Daton. I must confess your reputation precedes you. The reality is more than disappointing.'

'Likewise,' Daton said. 'Only thing is I've never heard of you.'

Mannix briefly closed his eyes. 'You went to a state comprehensive, did you not?'

Dates frowned. 'What does that have to do with anything?'

'I'm presuming you had a basic education?'

Dates nodded.

'So, you can read and write?'

'Yes. What's your point?'

Mannix sighed. 'My point is you asked for an explanation. And as my esteemed colleague pointed out, we left the manuscript at your disposal. All the answers laid in front of you.'

Dates raised her eyes. 'Yeah, I read it. I think it's as farfetched as a piece of shit from Mars, don't you?'

Mannix shot her a weak smile. It added no warmth to his countenance. Instead, it made him appear colder. 'Oh, I don't know. Is it any stranger than television or a man walking on the moon?'

'That's science,' Dates scoffed.

Mannix massaged his chin with his forefinger and thumb. '*New* science, this is old knowledge, lost wisdom plucked from our souls by fear and ignorance. Arcane, yes, but no less scientific. Just a different set of laws, that's all. Mysteries waiting to unfold. All you must do is believe.'

Dates rolled her eyes. 'I keep forgetting. I'm the new host.'

Mannix narrowed his eyes. 'Don't mock what you don't understand, girl. You're blessed to serve. Most would see what you'll give to the Order as an honour and a privilege.'

'And what is that exactly?'

Mannix and Quinby shared a glance. Then Quinby said, 'Time will reveal all.'

'That's the thing,' Dates said. 'Time's one thing I don't have.' She stepped closer and pressed her palms into the glass. 'You can't just kidnap people on a whim. Did it ever occur to you I have a contingency plan for stuff like this? People will come looking for me.'

'What people?' Mannix scoffed. 'From what Quentin tells me, you have no friends, and your fellow reprobates don't even like you. After that last fiasco, every pro refuses to work with you.'

Dates clenched her fists. 'Those people aren't worth knowing. It's true friends I'm talking about.'

Quinby laughed. 'Whom, a bunch of drunks who don't even know your name? Don't kid yourself. Although I agree, people are vile. Nobody cares where or who you are. And nobody's coming for you.'

Dates punched the glass directly in front of Quinby's face. Then struck it again, slowly at first, gaining momentum until blood smeared the spot and the pain stabbed at her knuckles, travelling through her arms as she lashed out with both fists. A voice screamed inside her head. The voice from the woods. Only it sounded different this time, more robust, more recognisable, blending with her own. Dates tried controlling her temper. Yet an irrepressible rage forced her on. It demanded she put an end to these lily-livered fools, urging her to scale the wall and punish these abhorrent self-serving men. She felt the anger blister inside her and, try as she might, failed to contain it.

Such disregard for her own life frightened her. Closing her eyes, she tried to compose herself. But the ringing in her ears and the sickness in her stomach made it impossible to think. Saliva flooded her mouth. Blood trickled from her nose, and the weakness surging through her body forced her to her knees. While the angry voices shouting her name grew distant, Dates tried to stand. She lacked the strength to get up, falling on her back. Her mistress's voice spiked with disappointment as she lost herself to the darkness.

2

She was neither awake nor asleep, a state of mind that enabled her consciousness to fuse with another's and drift. Freed from the body's shackles, her spirit, carried by a winter's airstream, floated above the corridors, curling through the gaps around the doors and coasting freely inside Quinby's lavish townhouse.

Engulfed in flames, the hot coals blazed from the marble fireplace. From a high back leather chair, Quinby studied Mannix, who stood facing him with his back turned to the window. Each man held a crystal wine glass, the grapey scent of an old Beaujolais mingling with the exquisite smokiness of two Cohiba Majestuosos cigars. It was a room heady with overindulgence, made more intoxicating by the men's bloated egos.

Dates settled behind Quinby's eyes. *Time to see the world from his side for once.*

Quinby rubbed his hand across his chest. This damned heartburn spoiled everything. His eyes stung like hell, the tiredness in his legs as persistent as the dull ache in his back. They were on their third bottle of wine, although looking at Mannix, one could easily assume the man hadn't touched a drop. No evidence of drink blotched his skin. His square shoulders rested on top of a straight back; the long legs looked solid, showing little signs of tiring.

'Everything all right, Quinby?' Mannix said. 'You look as though you want to say something.'

Quinby sipped his wine. 'I just recalled that previous incident with Dates. I knew she was a tough nut, but the way she pummelled into that glass appeared as though she was oblivious to the pain.'

Mannix didn't answer, his eyes fixed on his wine as he swirled it inside his glass. He continued to do this for a few seconds. Then, without looking up, he said, 'It's not her, of course; it's what's contained within.'

Quinby released an exasperated sigh. 'Yes, I know. That wasn't my point.'

'And what is your point?'

The two men stared at each other until Quinby said, 'That I'm apprehensive, yes, who wouldn't be. But I feel humbled by what the Order has agreed to bestow upon me. It's an honour and a privilege.'

This time it was Mannix who sipped his wine. And by the bitter look on his face, Quinby wondered if the vintage wasn't to his colleague's tastes.

'It was a close call,' Mannix said. 'The Order was divided on that. I'll not lie to you. I had hoped they would have favoured me, as a senior elder and all.'

Quinby smiled. 'You have no seniority here. This is my house, which reminds me of that little show of authority you performed today. It might impress a hired gun, but not me. Let's have no more of it.'

Mannix regarded him for a moment. 'You had little to say about it at the time. You seemed naturally subservient.'

Quinby placed his glass on the side table. 'Maturity of

mind is how I would describe it. The last thing we need is you and I bickering like two schoolboys.'

Mannix strolled towards him, placed his empty wine glass on the table, and sat in the chair opposite. Even the reflected flames failed to thaw the coldness in his eyes. His face looked crueller in the glowing firelight, and his long torso and broad shoulders cast an ominous shadow. Quinby had despised him since their first encounter. The doctor was conceited and aloof, attributes Quinby also possessed, although he recognised their limitations. Mannix's vanity made him vulnerable. Such a predilection for flattery made a man more open to mistakes. However, few shared Quinby's opinions. Most of the Order revered him. Even Quinby recognised the doctor's brilliance and vast knowledge of the ancients. Mannix had also complimented Quinby on his achievements. Although mutual respect and good manners made their time together tolerable, nothing could ever repair the deep rift between them.

Quinby gazed into the fire. 'The Order always has its divisions. I'm surprised you haven't tried to influence it.'

Mannix steepled his fingers while studying Quinby with those cold eyes, 'Who says I haven't?'

Quinby smiled to himself. 'Nobody, but I would have heard of it.'

'Are you sure?'

'As sure as I can be. Undeniably, you're the Order's *brightest star*. But some have other loyalties. Gratitude's in abundance when you're the keeper of so many dark secrets.'

Mannix regarded him for a moment. 'There's another side to that, of course.'

'Such as?'

'Keeping too many secrets can be dangerous. No one likes to be held to ransom. People become keen to get rid of you.' Mannix released a deep breath, then slapped his hands onto his lap. 'Yet it is in darkness where we reap, our nature, the Order demands it.' He smoothed a finger across his brow. 'Speaking of which, this Daton woman, you're confident she's fit for purpose?'

'She's certainly stronger than the other two.'

'She'll travel well?'

'Daton will be drugged. We'll have no trouble from her.'

Mannix pressed his lips into what could almost be described as a smile. 'I was referring to her sanity. Damaged goods might affect the ceremony.'

'That's extremely vigilant of you.'

Mannix straightened in his chair, his torso appearing larger. 'Not just that,' he said, with a grave look. 'There have been concerns, as you know.'

'About Daton?'

'Partly, but what alarms us more–'

'*Us?*'

'The *Order*. As I was saying, what worries us most is the whole debacle leading up to it.'

Quinby gripped his glass. 'It's hardly a debacle. Everything went according to plan.'

'Is that so because what happened in those Welsh woods can only be described as a *mess*.'

'Casualties for a higher cause.'

'Three dead bodies are hardly something that can pass by unnoticed.'

'Daton's a pro. I knew she would cover her tracks.'

Mannix sighed. 'Someone's bound to discover it, eventually. The last thing we need, especially at such a crucial time, is to bring attention to ourselves.'

Quinby smiled. 'You have more faith than I in our police force. There's no way they can trace it back to us.'

'What about that young girl's father?'

'*Jack Moran*,' Quinby scoffed. 'They found his van abandoned several weeks ago. Whatever happened to him remains a mystery.'

Mannix shot him an unconvinced look. 'Let's hope that's the case.'

Quinby did his utmost to remain stony-faced. His heart pounded inside his chest as Mannix's self-assured manner filled him with contempt. He knew Mannix's game. The envy lingered in his eyes, festering the moment the elders had chosen Quinby over him. For all his outward etiquette and style, Mannix lacked humility and grace. He viewed privilege as his sole right. Anyone else's good fortune was less deserving. He had wealth and influence, but Quinby had found the girl, and it was Quinby who would reap the rewards from offering Bathin the greatest sacrifice.

Mannix released a histrionic sigh, 'An exhausting day.'

Quinby nodded in agreement, 'And an early start tomorrow too.'

'Earlier for me, I'm afraid. I've business to attend to. I'll be travelling ahead of you.'

'What time do you need to leave? I'll have Christopher fix you some breakfast.'

Mannix scowled at the mention of the young man's name. 'Your private life is your own. But he'll have to attend the ceremony with the others. He can travel up with me if he likes. Until the ceremony's complete, you shouldn't be seen pampering him.'

'Chrissy took a beating from Daton. He's played a big part in making this happen. It's unfair to exclude him now.'

Mannix stood. 'I said nothing about excluding him, but he'll have to wait with the others while the elders prepare themselves. You and he must be separated.'

'Of course,' Quinby said. 'I've told him that. Several times. He doesn't like the idea but accepts it.'

Mannix regarded him for a moment. 'It's a dark path we

tread, Quentin; we all must make sacrifices; you, more than anyone, know there's no room for sentimentality.'

Quinby walked with Mannix into the hall and, having watched him ascend the stairs and satisfied he'd retired to his room, said, 'It's safe to come out now.'

Chrissy, dressed in silk white pyjamas, a glass of wine in one hand, a cigarette in the other, strolled towards him. Quinby scanned him with a disapproving eye. 'Why's your hair combed back like that? It makes you look older. I've told you before I don't like it.'

Chrissy pulled a face. 'Someone's in a foul mood. Did Dr Mannix upset you?'

Quinby shook his head. 'I've told you before about acting like this.'

'Like what?'

'Childish. You're always the same when you drink.'

Chrissy threw him an offended look. 'What else am I supposed to do. I'm not allowed to dine with you, be seen. I'm only good for one thing.'

Quinby smiled. 'Don't be like that.' He pointed to the lounge. 'Come and join me.' Chrissy followed him as requested. Yet when Quinby gestured for him to sit down, he refused. 'I've been sitting for hours. I prefer to stand, thank you.'

Chrissy stubbed out his cigarette, drank what remained of his wine and placed the empty glass on the side table. He stood behind Quinby's chair and began massaging his shoulders. Quinby let out a deep, contented sigh. 'You've a talent for knowing what I need, Chrissy.'

Chrissy undid the top buttons of Quinby's shirt and smoothed his soft, effeminate hand across his chest.

Quinby moaned. 'Those fingers are pure artistry.'

Chrissy's warm breath breezed across Quinby's neck. 'Better than your doctor friend?'

Quinby laughed. 'He's not that way inclined. Even if he were, he'd only have desires for himself.'

Chrissy moved his hand down further, stopping an inch above Quinby's waist. 'I heard him talking about me.'

Quinby opened his eyes, momentarily silenced by the beautiful young face gazing down at him. 'You have nothing to fear. Delusions of grandeur on his part. An alpha dog barking to establish his territory. Once it's done, I'll soon stop his whining. His meddling exhausts me. Don't worry. I'll deal with Mannix once it's all over.'

Chrissy giggled. 'I can't say I'll be sad to see Daton go.'

A pensive look travelled across Quinby's eyes. 'She's a character, that's for sure. But she used up all her chances after that last fiasco. At least she'll die for a bigger cause.' He reached up and touched Chrissy's shoulder. 'Let's speak of it no more. We have your career to look forward to. There's so much to think about.'

Chrissy knelt beside him, resting his head on Quinby's lap. Quinby stroked his hair, watching it gleam beneath the lamplight.

'Is Guy Bresson attending?' Chrissy said.

'Indeed, he is. Bresson's small potatoes at Pinewood. Bret De Angelo is your best bet. I'm told he's moved onto MGM.'

Chrissy pressed his cheek into Quinby's thigh. 'People have no idea what you're really like. You're not as bad as they say.'

Quinby laughed. 'I'm probably worse.'

Chrissy lifted his head and kissed Quinby's hand. 'You've shown me nothing but kindness.'

Quinby smiled. 'Yes,' he said, and after a long pause, added, 'no doubt it'll be the ruin of me.'

3

A sickening smell of petrol mixed with stagnant air hounded Dates for hours, and in the brief moments when she could open her eyes, she saw nothing but darkness. Her body, a leaden weight, remained helpless against the engine's relentless thrum while the incessant flow of traffic, washing over her, grew stronger whenever her thoughts fell silent.

She felt trapped in a journey that would never end. Yet when it did, her body remained lifeless.

They lifted her outside, the chilly winter air, like an ex-lover's kiss, passing cruelly across her skin while smells of wet pine and damp soil fused into a heady mix. Her body shivered, although, in this catatonic state, she could do nothing about it. She heard the crunch of gravel beneath their feet. Then as the air turned milder, the voices grew louder, amplified by what she imagined was an echoic hallway.

Her eyes opened periodically, catching glances of oak-panelled doors and large framed oil paintings lining the corridor walls. Then the light diminished as they descended a steep stairway, the narrow, dimly lit passage leading to a padded room, where they set her down on a cold mattress.

Dates lay still, gazing up at the immense, emblazoned symbol looming over her. At the symbol's centre was a crescent moon with a pair of winged demons standing on either side. She recognised it as the sign of the Order, knowledge obtained from observing the world through Quinby's eyes and the spirit that resided within.

⊂⊃

IN HER MIND'S EYE, Dates saw the faces of those who worshipped the great Duke Bathin and his master. As they had done for centuries, long before the Quinby's and Mannix's of this world, the privileged and the powerful, riddled with ambition and desire, assembled in a grotesque collective. A small group of men who, dissatisfied with their Masonic lodge, broke away to find the closed Order of the Crescent Moon, dedicated to studying the Cabbala, Hermetica and arcane Satanic texts. Among the subdued tones of distant chanting, she saw visions of sabbat rituals overseen by the hierarchy of the four elders. She felt the rivalries of weak men and inhaled the fear of their avowed followers.

Dates longed for it to be nothing more than a bad dream, yearning to awake, groggy and dry-mouthed in the smoke-filled comfort of Maggie's bar. Yet the nightmare was real, and any hint of her former life remained nothing but a distant memory.

Dates wiggled her toes, bending her fingers, inch by inch, until the tiredness passed through her. A constant pain throbbed inside her head, and although her legs and arms felt aged beyond their years, she managed to sit up. She combed a trembling hand through her hair, wincing at the greasy film across her fingers. She needed to remain focused. Fear was a given, and though proficient in using the adrenalin rush to her advantage, the odds were loaded against her.

Glancing down at her aching, swollen knuckles, Dates rubbed the blood away with her thumb. Those bastards hadn't even bothered to clean her up. She felt herself tense up, grinding her teeth while glancing around the padded cell.

With her energy returning, Dates stood, resting her back against the wall to balance herself. She scoured the cell for an opening. Nothing, not even a peep of light. Her stomach roared, and she couldn't recall the last time she ate. These fools seemed set on weakening her resolve, determined to starve her out.

Dates wondered what they'd done with her clothes as she stood there barefooted, dressed in what appeared to be a hospital gown. She tried reassuring herself that she'd gotten out of worse situations but failed to recall any. The key was to reserve her energy and seize any opportunity. They had to show themselves at some point.

Against all appearances, the padded cell wasn't soundproof. As the hours passed, she caught the sporadic sound of footsteps echoing down the passageway. She heard screaming too, faint at first, then becoming stronger, a tormented cry that broke into a desperate whimper. Dates called out to them, offering solace, hoping to find strength in numbers. 'What's your name?' she cried. 'Who are you? Do you know where we are?' She tried this for some time, but nobody answered.

Dates sat down, closed her eyes, and took a deep breath. For once, the voices in her head remained subdued, giving her a chance to think. Such calmness surprised her. She hadn't detached herself from its strangeness, just accepted the madness. The young travelling girl's image persisted in her mind's eye. Dates whispered her name. 'Hetty,' she repeated to herself, resolved to remember her as a person and not a human vessel to profit the likes of Quinby.

Dates still doubted Eves and Quinby's claims, although she found it difficult to deny the out-of-body experiences and this thing that dwelt inside her. An arcane sickness, perhaps? Whatever it was, the carnage was real, as was the trail of bodies it left behind. Eves and Casey's death wouldn't be the last; no, not if Dates had anything to do with it.

4

Dates stood among a small circle of trees, the frosty morning air prickling her skin. Lush grass swayed in the breeze, its scent so strong she could taste it. A teenage girl took her hand, her radiant smile matching her exuberant green eyes. It was a kind face. A face that glowed with the keen expectancy of youth.

A body lay face down in the grass, and Dates and the girl shared a glance of extreme sorrow. 'Her spirit now dwells with the trees,' Dates said as the presence's voice spoke from within her. 'Bathin asks us all for sacrifice, dearest daughter. She is at peace. All is for the greater good.'

Hand in hand, they ventured out from the confines of the trees, only turning to look behind them when they reached the path. Dates stared wistfully towards the Copse, cursing it before they left. The memory faded as towns and villages flashed intermittently in her mind's eye. She roamed from one body to the next, days turning into years, decades into centuries, her daughter's companionship and love filling her with immense joy.

Seabirds swooped across a cloudless blue sky, scavenging for food, their mewling cries sounding off towards the colossal passenger ship docked in the distance. Across the promenade, *weaving between the pedestrians and the horse-drawn buggies, Dates hurried towards it, 'Eme, Eme,' she cried, seeing her daughter in every stranger's face.*

She made it onto the pier, pushing through the crowd, hurrying towards the embarkment ramps, only stopping when a uniformed man stepped in front of her. 'Sorry, madam, you can't go any further; you'll need a ticket; they've started boarding.'

Dates tried pushing past, but the man, who was tall and heavyset, refused to budge. He fixed her with a stern eye. 'Please, madam, don't make matters difficult. You shan't pass without a ticket. Now, step back, or I'll call someone to remove you.'

'You don't understand,' Dates insisted. 'I need to speak with my daughter.'

The man sighed. 'You've had plenty of time for that. Now you better ....'

His words sank into the cacophony of distant voices while Eme, arm in arm with the man standing beside her, watched her from the upper decks. The sunlight reflecting off the water emphasized the smooth lustre of her skin. Her green eyes burned with childlike excitement, and Dates had seen no one so beautiful. The man was moustachioed with long sideburns, and Dates sensed overbearing neediness in his handsome face. 'Eme,' she cried. 'You vowed you'd stay. He's fickle and undeserving. Our bond is true, dearest Eme. Those lands are savage and cruel. You don't belong in such a place.'

A grey sky loomed above while the ship, the crowd, and Eme's bold smile melted around her. The voice inside Dates's head grew stronger. Rage and despair overwhelmed her.

On a blustery morning, she found herself on a beach, the seabirds scattering as the obscure figure approached her across the sands. 'This one's weak,' she murmured, and she saw the shore through the woman's eyes in a moment's breath. The woman's inner voice grew faint, the core of her, the essence that made her unique, reduced to nothing, as though her soul was eternally lost.

The notion was so terrifying that it forced Dates to her feet. Shaken and dry-mouthed, she paced her cell; her hands clenched tightly into fists, the aftertaste of those visions lingering like a nasty smell.

Those memories were hers now. Together with the shame and regret for the young girl who lay comatose in the hospital, Dates now yearned for a missing daughter and grieved for a dead girl in the woods. They slid beneath her skin, skulking with her own, feelings so intense they left an insatiable emptiness inside her.

Dates pressed her fingers to her temples as the whispers inside her head grew stronger. No wonder Casey went insane. Hetty Moran, Ida Parry, and those who came before them were too weak to withstand this madness. Not that Dates was any exception. But she sure as hell was going to try.

5

Four men entered the cell; three waited in the corridor while Dates, exhausted and half-starved, readied herself for the fight. Two of the men held a control pole. One sought to place the noose over her head, and the other her leg, seeking to ensnare her like a wild animal. On a full belly and armed with her High-Power, the situation would have posed little threat. But she was tired and weak, a voice screeching in her head, the odds clearly stacked against her.

A tall, wiry man made his move and Dates dropped him with a sudden kick. Another man came at her from the side, and while she grappled him to the floor, she felt a noose tighten around her neck, pulling her back. She gripped it with both hands and tried loosening it from her throat, the thin plastic cord slicing into her fingers. The harder she tried, the more it tightened. A bald, pockmarked man tried to grab her foot. Dates kicked out, regretting it when the second noose looped around her ankle.

'Got the bitch,' someone cried, and after one mighty tug, Dates lay on her back.

Those watching from the corridor charged inside.

Cowards, every one of them, brave in numbers, feeding off a weakened prey. They held her down and bound her feet and hands. She struggled as best she could, spitting and cursing until they gagged her mouth. They carried her into the corridor, the air a foul blend of vomit and excrement, the remnants of her fellow damned or the wretched soul in the next cell.

From the cellar depths, they entered the great hall, the heraldic stained-glass windows covered to shut out the light. Oil lanterns dangled from the walls, burning brightly, their flames reflected across the polished oak floor, and through the gaps in the curtains shone hints of moonlight. Men and women, joining hands, formed a large circle around the hall's perimeter. They looked bloated and middle-aged, overly made-up women with poodle perms and moustachioed men with long sideburns. They stood naked and aloof, their skin leathered and gravy-brown from long idle days beneath a foreign sun.

In the northern part of the hall stood a candlelit altar with a satin cloth draped over it; a long, white-handled knife was placed in its centre with a silver chalice beside it. Watching over them was a stone sculpture of a serpent-tailed man on horseback. Dates recognised the fierce demonic face from a dream, although no dream compared to the nightmarish reality of this.

Incense burners hung on either side of the altar. Fragrant smoke clouds lingered; their violet-laced perfume was sweet and sickly. In front of the altar, on the floor, was a large, elaborately painted heptagram. Symbols populated its outer circle, and in its centre, above a gold crescent moon, stared an omniscient dark eye.

They propped Dates up against the wall, the circle parting, as a robed Mannix, with Quinby and two other men at his side, walked ceremoniously to the altar. Mannix lay face down within the heptagram, his arms spread above his head. He remained there for some time, the congregation watching him in silence.

Mannix pushed himself onto his knees and stretched his arms towards the altar. 'Hail to the Duke Bathin. From the abodes of night, we seek thy praise, and I lowly kneel before thee. I adore thee to the end, and with loving sacrifice thy shrine adorns; my lips are top thy feet; my prayer upon the rising incense smoke descends to aide me; without thee I am lonely, a feeble man with none to guide me.'

Mannix stood motionless while Quinby and the other men removed his outer robe. He took the knife from the altar, then the chalice with his other hand, and dressed only in white smocks, all four men turned to face the congregation.

Mannix held out the chalice and placed the knife inside it. 'As the cup is to woman, so is the knife to man.'

'And in truth, let them be united,' everyone said in unison.

Mannix smiled, then handed the chalice to the man on his right. He glanced about the room, an intensity in his dark eyes as he acknowledged each awestricken face. 'This is a momentous day. On such a day, we must remind ourselves of the universal laws that guide us. When we join the Order, we are made aware of the four elements that form the universe: water, earth, air, and fire. These elements serve to remind us. They awaken us to ourselves; they show us our base fears: water, our fear of drowning, air, our fear of being lost, earth, our fear of being entombed, and fire, our fear of pain. We must always endeavour to master these fears, or we are incapable of wisdom. Yet such fears also remind us we are weak. Our Lord Duke Bathin demands we remain humble. Without humility, our offerings are worthless and thus will remain unrewarded.'

Mannix gestured for Quinby to step forward. 'Move into the circle, learned friend.'

Quinby, with all the pomp and pretension the moment allowed, stepped forward. He looked ludicrous in his white smock. His rubicund cheeks and protruding belly gave him the look of an overaged choirboy. Even in her most desperate hour, Dates longed to wipe the smug look from his face. A face that was bloated and overindulged as eager ambition blazed in his devious eyes. She didn't have to wait, the shock in Quinby's eyes matching her own as a naked Chrissy was dragged into the hall.

Bloodied and bruised, a hunched Chrissy stumbled into the centre circle. He dropped to his knees, grabbed Quinby's ankles, and pushed his lips to his lover's feet. 'Please, Quentin,' he pleaded, 'please.' He raised his head. 'What's happening, Quentin? Please, make it stop. The things these people have done to me.' He broke into a sob as the memory of such vile acts overwhelmed him. 'Make it stop, Quentin,' he begged. 'You promised great things. I don't deserve this.'

'What we deserve,' Mannix said, 'is for Bathin alone to decide.' He gave Quinby a scathing glance. 'Carnal lusts cannot impede these sacred rites. Desire makes our offerings impotent. True sacrifice shows our humility, acknowledges our weaknesses, and only through that may we bathe in Bathin's light.' Mannix looked down at Chrissy, the coldness in his eyes unflinching. He looked up and turned towards Quinby. 'Do you deny Bathin his true spoils? I know you have feelings for the poor creature who kneels before us. But this is *your* time. And this is *your* test.'

Quinby appeared lost for words, and Dates wondered if he would intervene. Would that solitary grain of feeling suddenly declare itself? She studied the shine in Quinby's eyes, watching it fade until his face wore its usual impassive mask. 'To serve Bathin is my only purpose,' he said, oblivious to Chrissy's screaming.

Chrissy's protests were short-lived. The bald, pock-marked man stepped out from the circle, grabbed Chrissy by the hair, yanked back his head and cut his throat. Shock flashed in Chrissy's eyes, and then he collapsed, face down, in his own blood.

Quinby fixed Mannix with an icy glare. 'It's done; now let's get on with it.'

Mannix gave him a sanctimonious smile. 'Patience, friend, there is one more test.'

With his hands outstretched, Mannix stood facing the congregation. 'Our learned friend has shown his willingness to appease our Lord Duke. Yet, we must bestow him with a greater gift before receiving his blessing.' He turned his head slightly and motioned Quinby to join him at his side. Quinby did as he was asked, looking more grieved with every reluctant step. Mannix fixed him with a cold eye. 'Today was to be your time. However, you must further prove your humility and relinquish that right.'

'Nonsense,' Quinby shouted. 'Outrageous, nonsense.' He squared up to Mannix. 'I'll do no such thing. This is–'

'Enough,' Mannix said, placing a hand on Quinby's chest. 'You'll do as the Lord Duke Bathin wishes. The Order has decided.'

'*When?*'

'For some time. Your weaknesses have been noted. I tried warning you. I even advised we test you first to give you the benefit of the doubt.'

'Nonsense.' Quinby protested. 'Utter nonsense. I deserve this. This isn't for any greater good. These are the treacherous acts of a–'

'Of a what?' Mannix interrupted. 'A conceited man?' He glanced around the room, all eyes upon him, wide with expectation, every gluttonous smile feasting on the fight. 'Witness our learned friend's response,' Mannix said. 'And ask yourself, is this the reaction of a selfless, humble man, or a man who covets Bathin's grace, not for the greater good of the Order, but for self-empowerment and his own vices?'

'Selfish,' someone cried. 'Ignoble,' said another, the circle muttering among themselves, all eyes brimming with accusation, all heads appearing to move in one consensual nod.

Mannix glanced up at the window. 'We have little time,' he said, his words causing the room to fall silent. 'I am but a humble man. I take guidance from you all, and the Order has decreed that should our learned friend fail us, which he undoubtedly has, I should take his place.'

The instant Quinby stepped forward, Mannix nodded towards the circle. The bald, pockmarked man, accompanied by a taller, oafish-looking brute, tapped Quinby's arm and guided him away. Quinby stood among the congregation, his face blending with the other onlookers until he was lost within the hall's darkness. Dates had often pictured Quinby's downfall. She'd imagined enjoying a brutal, prolonged battle, which would see her as triumphant. Yet the mundanity of his humiliation and the defeated look in his eyes would always deprive her of that. Not that she had time to dwell on it. No sooner had Quinby been brushed aside than Mannix ordered them to 'bring the woman forward.'

6

They carried Dates into the circle, dumping her onto the floor as though she was nothing more than a joint of tied beef. It took three men to unbind her hands and three more to untie her feet. The bald, pockmarked man sliced through her gown, hacking it away from her body until she lay naked. She felt the cold air fall across her chest, the men gripping her tighter, their warm, clammy hands slickening her skin with sweat.

Dates breathed hard and fast, trying not to panic as the incense-laced air burned inside her throat. She shut her eyes. If there was ever a need to invoke Helenora Haye's spirit, it was now. Dates tried picturing all those inherited memories, opening herself up to the voices.

The congregation drew closer and formed a tighter circle around her. Mannix stepped inside, carrying a silver bowl, and placed it on the floor. He knelt over it and drew some water out with his cupped hands. Then stood, sprinkling water around the heptagram's outer circle. He knelt back down, his long, bony finger tracing the shape of a pentagram across Dates's bare chest. While Dates lay spread-eagled on the floor, Mannix removed his smock and lay on top of her, pressing his face into her neck and holding it there among the monotonous incantations.

Mannix stood, naked and aroused, his hands raised above his head. 'As I prepare to pass from this self and embrace the next, I feel Bathin's presence. I trust that in aught I do, he is with me. He abides in me, and I in him. No misfortune shall I endure, for the dweller that passes from this body unto mine abides to my bidding and to thine will. For humility and servitude do I strive, and as I spill the blood of the vessel which lies before me, let the spirit pass unto mine own as is Bathin's will.'

As though Duke Bathin himself had answered Mannix's decree, the sound of gunshot cracked through the air like thunder. The outer circle dispersed. Yet the men who held Dates down remained, staring at each other with startled, questioning faces while the congregation fell into disarray.

Mannix, now covered in his smock, appealed for calm. 'Remain as you are,' he said. He turned towards Quinby. 'Step down, man, step down. Don't make this any worse for yourself.'

Quinby answered with his customary pompous smile. 'You've given enough orders for today. You seem to forget who's holding the gun.'

Mannix glared at him. 'And what do you intend to do with it?'

'Take control for one.' He nodded towards Dates. 'You can release her for a start.'

'Why would we do that? It will be months or even a year before we get another chance.'

'*We?*' Quinby said. 'Don't you mean *you*? Oh, I forgot, you're far too selfless for that. I'm the conceited one.'

Mannix looked towards the bald, pockmarked man standing beside him. 'Disarm this maniac,' he said through an exasperated sigh.

Quinby raised his gun, 'I wouldn't advise that,' he said, calmly shooting the man in the head the instant he stepped forward. The bald, pockmarked man crumpled into a heap, Mannix's instant rebuke drowned out by the screams and shouts. Quinby didn't waste any time, ordering the men, who still had hold of Dates, to free her immediately.

Dates leapt up from the floor like a wild cat sprung from its cage. She pulled the gag from her mouth, light-headedness dulling her thoughts while she waited for the circulation to return to her hands and feet.

The frightened look in her oppressors' eyes was a fierce contrast to the gluttonous self-pride that preceded it. They scattered in droves. Some of them squatted down on the floor, holding their head in their hands. Others wept and moaned, and in these trying moments, it wasn't Bathin who they implored for help, but 'Jesus,' they cried. 'God, please save us,' turning their backs on the darkness and seeking refuge in the light.

Quinby fired another shot, dispelling those still foolish enough to approach. He offered Dates his hand. 'Come on, let's go.'

Dates shook her head. 'I'm not going anywhere with you.'

'For God's sake, woman. Come on. I'm your best chance at the moment. You can settle old scores later. Come on, Daton. Let's go before they have time to arm themselves.'

Dates looked at him askance, mindful of the congregation as they fled around her. 'Where are my clothes?' she asked, suddenly aware of her nakedness.

Quinby responded with an indignant shrug. 'How on earth should I know? Surely, that's the least of your worries.'

'All my worries are down to you.' She considered kicking the gun from his hand, breaking his neck with one swift twist. Quinby didn't deserve a quick death. He was right, of course. He was her best bet if she wanted to get away from this place. But once they were clear from harm's way, she didn't rate Quinby's chances of survival. He might have been lucky enough to smarm his way out of this one. But if Dates had anything to do with it, the odds were stacked firmly against him.

She accompanied him out of the hall, hurrying along the darkened corridors, feeling the cold wooden floor beneath her feet. Quinby pointed to a makeshift cloakroom. 'Everyone's clothes are over there. Find something, and let's go.'

Dates scanned him with a disapproving eye. 'And you?'

'What about me?'

'You're going to drive us to London in a smock?'

The expression on Quinby's face was almost a smile. He followed Dates into the cloakroom, snatched his clothes from the rack and slipped into a booth to dress.

'Shy,' Dates shouted while she rummaged through the racks. 'I think you're well beyond preserving any dignity.' She found a pair of jeans to fit, a checked shirt, and a pair of low-heeled boots. Quinby appeared from the booth as though he was about to attend an evening recital. He wore a burgundy blazer with a black turtleneck and matching slacks.

'Why are you helping me?' Dates asked. 'You and I are finished. You owe me more than a hefty sum. If we survive this, things won't go well for you when we get back.'

Quinby reloaded his gun. 'Presently, you're my closest ally, which is no compliment to you, but a reflection on the direness of the situation.'

'I might just go off alone.'

'I wouldn't advise that. Bathin's been summoned. You'll need someone with you when the voice calls within.'

Dates frowned. 'What voice?'

Quinby didn't answer, silenced by the sudden sound of footsteps running down the corridor. 'We need to go.'

Dates gestured towards the gun. 'Why not give that to me. I could make better use of it.'

'I'd be dead the moment it touched your hand.'

'In usual circumstances, yes. But, until you've paid me, I'll deprive you of the pleasure of death.'

Quinby hesitated for a second, then handed Dates the gun. She breathed deeply, relishing the grip on her hand. It was no match for her Hi-Power, but now it was the next best thing. 'Bullets?'

Quinby tapped his pocket. 'We've a few rounds, although I don't recommend wasting them.'

Dates pointed the gun at Quinby's head and watched him pale. 'Oh, have no fear of that. I don't intend to.'

7

Quinby led the way, guiding them past the pantry, across the kitchen, and then outside, hurrying their pace as they followed the path next to the garden wall. Dates had lost all sense of time. Yet, judging by the moonlit sky and the gloomy darkness surrounding the faraway trees, she sensed it was past midnight. They broke into a jog, the distant voices drawing closer. Dates stopped, gripping the gun with both hands, and pointed it towards the house.

'What on earth are you doing?' Quinby asked.

Dates remained focused on the house. 'I'm not running from these fools. A few direct hits, and they'll scatter like the cowards they are.'

Quinby sighed. 'A little reckless, don't you think? The best thing for us to do is leave. I thought you, of all people, would have known that. Did you learn nothing from your last fiasco?'

When Quinby turned around, Dates pointed the gun at his back. It wouldn't take much effort to pull the trigger. She would feel so much better and save a host of unfortunate souls from years of misery. She pictured the young girl lying quietly in the hospital bed. Money was no recompense for a life lived in purgatory. But at least it was something. A modest offering to show her remorse. The only gesture that made all this madness seem worth it.

Once they reached the large, gravelled driveway, Quinby pointed at a racing-green Triumph Stag Convertible. He dashed towards it, swung open the driver's door and sat inside. 'The village is just over twenty miles. She'll have us there in no time.'

Dates climbed into the passenger seat. 'Makes little sense to stop. Let's just hit the motorway.'

Quinby placed the key into the ignition and started the engine. 'We need to fill the tank,' he said patronisingly. 'Besides, once we're in the village, no one would dare harm us.'

'No one will harm us now. They were running scared the last time I looked.'

Quinby shifted into reverse, manoeuvring the car onto the track with one swift glance over his shoulder. 'Mannix has his guards. Loyal to the bone. They'll help until their last breath.' He glanced into the rear-view mirror. 'He doesn't take failure lightly. You've witnessed first-hand the lengths we're prepared to go to. Mannix refuses to let such an opportunity slip.' Quinby pressed down on the accelerator, shifting through the gears, and raced towards the main gates.

It came as no surprise to find the gates locked. Quinby flashed Dates one of his looks. 'You'll need to do the honours, I'm afraid. Slip the chain from the bar and once I've driven through, ensure you put it back.'

Dates returned Quinby's look with one of her own, hopped out of the car and took to the task without argument. The chain was heavier than she expected. She tugged at it, using all her strength to free it from the latch. It dropped to the ground with a thud, like a rusty, coiled snake hiding in the wet grass. She stepped aside while Quinby drove through, catching sight of two Land Rovers speeding towards them.

Dates got back into the car. 'What?' she said in reply to Quinby's disapproving look.

Quinby shook his head. 'Do you intend to put that chain back and lock the gate?'

Dates pointed ahead. 'Drive. That chain wasn't keeping it locked. They'd be right behind us by the time I'd faffed about with it.

Quinby pressed down on the accelerator, the car juddering intermittently as they drove down the long, potholed track. The trail cut through the tall trees; the moonlight veiled behind the dense woodland on either side.

'Get a move on,' Dates said, then squinted at the bright flash of headlights. The car gained speed as an expression of dark determination settled on Quinby's face.

'Slow down,' Dates insisted, 'you'll give us a flat.'

Quinby didn't respond. He stared at the road, seeming set on crashing into the vehicle driving towards them.

Dates pressed the gun against Quinby's temple. 'Slow down, I said.'

Quinby eased off the accelerator. 'Your reluctance surprises me. It's a simple game of chicken. They'll swerve once we get closer.'

'Sometimes, you're quite stupid for an educated man. They've no intention of moving.' She peered over her shoulder. 'Neither have these clowns behind us. All they want is to wedge us in.'

Quinby sighed. 'And what do you suggest we do?'

'Stop the car. Our best option, for now, is in those woods. We've a better chance if we draw them out.'

'Don't talk so stupid.'

'Have you ever been in a car crash, Quinby?'

Quinby shook his head.

'No. I thought not. Well, I can assure you it's not a pleasurable experience. A sudden shock to the system, pained, confused, and that's without the addition of these goons firing at us.'

'That's not going to happen. Well, not for now, at least. For the next few hours, they need you in one piece.'

'I'm not going to allow that. I'm staying out in the open. I've had my fill of confined spaces.' She forced the gun harder against the side of Quinby's head. 'Now stop the car. I've no intention of asking again.'

Quinby slammed down on the brakes, coming to a sudden stop. Dates swung open the car door and stepped outside. At first, Quinby refused to budge, then he killed the engine and followed her into the trees.

PART V

FROM WITHIN THE TREES

1

Quinby kept asking what she planned to do next, and Dates, crouching down with her back against a tree, told him, 'I'm going to wait.'

'Wait, for what specifically?' Quinby said through a sigh. 'For them to come charging into the woods so you can gun them down one by one?'

Dates wiped the sweat from her brow. 'Yeah, something like that.'

'That's not going to happen. Mannix is too clever.' He glanced up at the moon, then gave Dates a pensive look. 'All he need do is wait, and not too long by the look of you.'

'What's that supposed to mean?'

'If we had a mirror, I'd show you.' He slid his hand into his jacket pocket and drew out his lighter. He flipped open the cap, ignited it, and brought the flame close to Dates's face. 'Your eyes look a little bloodshot, and your skin has a nice tinge of grey.'

Dates slapped the lighter from his hand. 'Put that thing out. You'll lead them straight to us. Or is that what you want?'

'Of course, it isn't. What kind of man do you think I am?'

Dates looked Quinby fiercely in the eyes. 'We all know the kind of man you are, Quinby. If Chrissy were still alive, he'd testify to that.'

Quinby didn't answer. Not that he needed to. Any response he could offer was best said by the ensuing silence.

Dates listened to the Land Rovers' distant roar. Their headlights splintered through the trees. Men's voices carried on the night air, and the slamming of car doors was followed by relentless barking. Dates threw Quinby an inquisitive look.

'A guard dog from the far gates,' Quinby said as though reading her mind. 'German Shepherd, handsome brute, undoubtedly they'll send the poor creature to sniff you out.'

'Dogs aren't as fearless as folk think. I won't hurt it if I can avoid it. One shot should be enough to scare it off.'

Feeling lightheaded, Dates struggled to stand, her limbs shaky, as though something was sucking the life from her. She closed her eyes for a second and took a deep breath, trying to gain clarity of thought; another voice whispered inside her head, that old familiar, pestering, determined to drown out her own.

She opened her eyes to an assault of torch lights. Each beam shone into the darkness, resting intermittently as they combed the trees. Quinby clutched her arm and tried forcing her deeper into the woods. Dates stayed put, her reluctance to leave growing stronger. A belligerent determination rooted her to the ground. She gripped her gun, pointing it towards the dog's barking.

When Quinby loosened his grip, Dates didn't bother to look over her shoulder. She liked the idea of him not being around. His sudden absence was like a spell of fresh air. Sadly, it was a brief respite, the aroma of the trees marred by the sickening smell of sweat and cheap aftershave as Mannix and his henchmen drew closer.

A dog's shadow weaved through the trees, the brute's suppleness and grace highlighting the rigidity of its masters. Snarling and with ears pricked, it darted towards her. Dates fired a shot into the air, stopping the dog in its tracks. It studied her momentarily, the caution in its eyes quickly fading. The dog edged closer, snarled, and leapt at her chest. Dates was just as quick, slipping her hand into the dog's gaping mouth, snatching its tongue, knowing the poor animal wouldn't bite down on it. She twisted its tongue, nothing too severe, just enough to send the poor creature off yelping.

Dates slunk back further into the trees, beyond the reach of the torchlights. She heard the men rush forward, her heartbeat growing thicker as the twigs and dead branches snapped beneath their feet. The voices inside her head forced her eyes to shut as the lingering damp air, fused with the stench of rotten leaves, grew more intoxicating. Dates felt her body lean to the left, and seconds later, she was on her back.

In a fit of panic, she gripped the gun tighter, digging her heels into the wet soil, managing to push herself backwards and lean her weight into a tree. She failed to open her eyes, inner screams of frustration suppressed by someone shouting. A herd of worms twisted and crawled in her mind's eye, moist and long, writhing among a bed of earth, feasting on a mulch of decayed animal remains, mould, fungi, and dead plants, squirming beneath her, their pulpy, regurgitated ooze seeping into her skin.

Behind her closed eyelids, she saw the orange glare of the torchlights. They shone warmly upon her face, instantly retracting when Dates, like a blind man warding off intruders, aimlessly pointed her gun.

Their voices drew closer, and she sensed them form a circle around her.

'We'll finish it here,' Mannix said. 'There's no time to move her.'

The words clawed at her soul, and her body, rooted to the earth, remained powerless against them. Dates fired two shots; the gun kicked from her hand before she could fire a third.

2

They saw no reason to restrain her. Paralysed from the waist down, Dates lay outstretched while they cut and tore off her clothes. The jumble of voices morphed into a chant. Its monotonous rhythms vibrated through her bones while the voice inside her head screamed in defiance.

A cluster of images flashed in her mind's eye: *A condemned woman in a cell drew solace from her daughter's love. Two figures gazed earnestly at the body in the grass, taking no comfort from its hollow shell. Black-eyed crows conspired among the trees, and the river flowed east, carrying a current of lost dreams and unheard voices. A beak pecked at a vagabond's eye. Shells whispered a thousand mysteries, travelling on the breeze as a woman, clad in Victorian clothes, consoled a stranger wandering along the sands. A queen reigned, the worms turned, and the crows descended on those reluctant to serve. That insatiable feeling of loss lasted ten lifetimes. Then a rudiment of hope surfaced upon the plains. A young woman, wiser than her years, took them home. A snare snapped the quarry's neck. Blood flows from the avarice of lesser men; blood flows when the weak answer Bathin's call.*

Mannix scanned her shape, his stare lingering too long. The knife flashed in the torchlight, Dates's body unflinching until the blade pierced her skin. A look of satisfaction settled in Mannix's eyes, the steady expression of reticence and calm tarnished by greed and more than a hint of madness. He sank his finger into the trickle of blood and smeared it across her chest. Dates reached out her hand. 'Rest, child,' he said calmly. 'Bathin hears our call.'

She murmured something, and Mannix answered with a slight bow of the head. 'The time for words is over, child. Be silent, let the darkness ....'

Dates grabbed a fistful of Mannix's hair, savouring his look of astonishment as she yanked his face down onto her knee. She quickly positioned herself beneath him, his body covering her like a second skin. She placed the knife to his throat, guns clicking in retaliation, but as she lowered the blade to the nape of Mannix's back, no one dared to fire a shot.

Dates ordered Mannix to stand, which he did without question; his stance laboured and stooped as his trembling body pressed against her. Dates remained still, breathing in unison with the rise and fall of his chest. She felt like an onlooker, a voyeur, watching the events unfold through the distance of a bad dream.

'Listen, my child,' Mannix whispered, falling silent when Dates plunged the knife into his back.

Mannix's gun weighted comfortably against her palm as her fingers tightened around its grip. A bullet ripped into someone's skull, another tore into the heart, and a kneecap shattered, splattering the soil with blood and flesh. Dates glimpsed the deadness in the eyes of the fallen, then slipped back into the trees, curtailing the swiftness of their attack.

They chased after her into the woods, their frantic shouts ringing through the trees, fearful, bitter men firing aimlessly into the darkness. Skulking confidently among the dead leaves, Dates relished the coolness against her skin. She was the huntress of the hunters, a divine assassin, following the shadows of her prey through the soft spills of moonlight.

Watching the night through Helenora's eyes, she saw all that was hidden in the darkness. Weevils and sap-sucking aphids feasted on the leaves; moths basked in the flickers of light; worms turned the soil; powderpost beetles and carpenter ants skittered silently across the grass.

One of Mannix's gun-toting brutes crossed her path, and she ended his days with a sharp twist of the neck. The others grew more discrete, biding their time, watching, waiting, infecting the night with each fear-laden breath. Someone shot a flare into the sky, its brilliant red flame lingering above the trees before melting into the darkness.

'She's at seven o'clock,' someone shouted, drawing them out from their hiding place. They fired relentlessly at the trees, seeking refuge in numbers. Dates hunkered down behind a thick, dead oak, only firing when she had a clear shot. She caught one in her sights, watching the bloody mass of sclera, pupil, and iris explode from what had once been his left eye.

This was Dates at her best, gunning them down, shooting one in the chest, another in the head, and the third in the belly while he snaked coweringly through the wet grass.

Only two of Mannix's henchmen remained, oblivious to their master's cries for help and the sound of hooves clip-clopping towards them in the distance. The survivors, for that's all they were, appeared resolute to go the whole course. They lay behind a barricade of fallen trees, the cold night air carrying their every whisper.

Dates edged forward, her pale, naked body weaving

through the woods like an avenging ghost. She felt like a passenger in her own body, the strangest feeling, more of a witness than an executioner, her inner voice growing more distant.

Dates stepped softly, pushing her toes through the sodden leaves while the soles of her feet trod indifferently across the prickly twigs and the stone-infested grass. A man peeped from his cradle of trees, fixing Dates in his sights, his eyes shining with a sense of victory. The moment was short-lived. Dates leapt over the fallen trees, the man unable to turn and fire before she slit open his belly with her knife. He stared in awe at his spilt guts. Terror settled in his eyes. A look Dates had seen so often when folk realised the imminence of their own death.

The other man had more luck; he fired wildly in Dates's direction, dropping her to her knees as a bullet skimmed her shoulder. Immense pain surged through her bones, then a sudden numbness kicked in, and the agony abated. Dates didn't lose any time. As the man fumbled to reload, she got up and jabbed his jaw. Unaffected, he seized her wrists and dragged her towards him, head-butting the bridge of her nose, the plastic-like smell of his polyester bomber jacket mingling with the smell of blood and sweat. He tried forcing her to the ground, but Dates was too quick, slipping her foot behind his leg and dropping him onto his back. The man reached for his knife. 'Crazy bitch, you crazy fu–' falling silent when Dates grabbed his gun and fired it into his mouth.

Dates felt so tired, yet the image of the girl stopped her from sinking into non-existence. Watching her lie senseless in her hospital bed, Dates had never seen innocence so personified as it was in that sweet young face. She slept like an angel, shrouded in her white gown, breathing in unison with the sound of the ventilator.

Dates stood, that recognisable determination enabling her to hold on to a part of herself. She needed to get home, get the money owed to her and help the girl as best she could. It was the only thing to cling to, a distant star in the darkness that made all this madness seem worth it.

A persistent cry for help grew louder until falling silent at the sound of a gunshot. Someone called her name. 'Daton. Daton. Daton, where are you?'

She followed it through the woods, stopping when she saw Quinby's moonlike face staring at her through the half-darkness.

Mannix's dead body lay at Quinby's feet. Quinby flashed her a callous smile. 'You severed the poor man's spinal cord. He couldn't walk.' He nodded at the gun in his hand. 'I found it in the grass. I watched him suffer for a while. But even a heart as cold as mine felt compelled to put him out of his misery.' He cast Dates a disapproving look. 'We need to get you dressed. You look awful even by your standards.' He studied her for a moment. 'Let's get you back home before you're completely lost to us.' Avarice gleamed in his eyes. 'Something good might still come of this.'

Dates crumpled to the ground, her legs lifeless, her chest tightening as she battled to catch her breath. Stars twinkled in the clearing sky as a horse's elongated shadow swept across her in the moonlight. Her heart pulsed inside her ears and throat, and she felt the last shreds of herself fading. *Get up*, she cried from the infinite blackness. *Stay awake*, she screamed again and again. Her voice became distant and weak, smothered by another's presence, trapped inside a body that demanded sleep.

3

She awoke dressed in a man's overcoat, still cold to the bone, and her hair soaked through. From the car window, she watched the low fog draped above the trees unfurl lazily across the grass. The road, vacant of traffic, cut through the endless stretches of moorland. No birds flew across the murky sky, yet she sensed them watching her from their quiet confinement.

Much to her annoyance, Quinby was less discrete, turning up the volume on the radio while a 50s Jazz ditty played on. The piece was bearable if left alone. Quinby made it intolerable, a tuneless rendition that he whistled tirelessly through his teeth. He must have felt her glare because he turned his head towards her, the whistling, thankfully, ending abruptly. 'Finally awake,' he added with a smirk. 'I thought I might have overdone the dosage, feared we'd lost you.'

He set his eyes on the road. 'You'll find it'll subdue you for a while, that and what stirs within.' He threw her another smile. A smile she recognised from old. A smile she'd seen so many times before whenever a man felt pleased with himself.

'There was a point in those woods where I'd suspected all was lost,' Quinby said. 'I've dreamt of this moment for years. Defeat lurks among the weak-willed. Folk like us can always find a way. We've the strength to dig deep.' He cast her an amused smile. 'I warned you about that conscience of yours.' He released an exaggerated sigh. 'But much to my astonishment, I will actually miss you, Dates, when it's all over.'

She'd always despised the name. But what provoked her more was how he used it with such contemptuous familiarity. She watched him intently for over thirty minutes, only averting her gaze when he pulled up to fill the car with petrol.

Being the only garage for miles, unsurprisingly, there was a queue. She shuffled in her seat, surreptitiously raised her hand, and unclipped her seatbelt. She watched the people for a minute, gazing upwards when she grew bored with their tired, impatient faces.

Few clouds marred the midday sky; the dawn fog was nothing but a distant memory. A line of birds flew east, descending into a cloud of blue-grey. She could have stared at the clouds for hours, mesmerized by the faces she saw within them. She saw an old man; his eyes were wicked, and no smile graced his grim, bearded face. He triggered memories of darker times, and then she forgot him in the passing of a sigh.

Her gaze wandered over the clouds. The yearning inside her grew stronger, deepening as her eyes settled on a young woman's face. For centuries, the sceptics and disbelievers claimed we see what we want to. But she'd learned enough about the world to know that wasn't the case. Nature's mysteries were untold. The light and the darkness taught you nothing was a coincidence, especially once you'd had a taste.

She shut her eyes to suppress the longing inside her. It was a centuries-old pain, one love-struck girl's foolish mistake, followed by years of searching. She breathed deeply. Then, as Quinby swung open the car door, she opened her eyes.

'Apologies for the long wait. I'm amazed anyone would venture out to this godforsaken place, let alone on the same day.' His breath was sour, which, coupled with the dank smell of his clothes, gave him an odour that often accompanied the unwashed. He caught her look of disdain and rebuked it with his own. 'Peasants,' he growled, slotted the key into the ignition and started the engine. He shifted into first, keeping his hand on the gear stick as he glanced down at her seatbelt. 'That's odd; I could have sworn I....'

She leaned forward and pressed her mouth to his ear, whispering each word as she'd done to so many others before him. Quinby recoiled in surprise and opened his mouth to say something but remained silent.

Helenora studied him with an amused smile. 'What is the land without a queen to reign and a worm to serve and turn the earth?' she whispered.

The defiance in Quinby's eyes vanished, replaced by a blank expression of absolute subservience. It was a look she had seen so many times before. A look which, until he served no purpose, was forever his.

WITCHES COPSE CONTINUES ...

WITH THE FORTHCOMING WITCHES BLOODING

Read the sample chapter

Also check out the **FREE** Witches Copse insights, stories, **podcast** and articles in the **Into the Witches Copse** section of my **Newsletter.** You can also subscribe to the newsletter to get the latest updates on Free stories and flash fiction, plus news, updates, articles, and insights on my current and forthcoming books.

https://mathbird.substack.com

WITCHES BLOODING
SAMPLE CHAPTER

THE JOURNAL OF EME CAMPBELL

Asherfield County 1896

M*arch 16, 1896 -*

AFTER EXPRESSING my anxiety about starting our new life, Stuart suggested I release my demons to the page. He said I should record our new adventure from its outset, adding that our ghosts are more easily tamed when we confine them with pen and paper. The sentiment, as with everything Stuart does, was well-intended. He read my reluctance as a shyness to disclose; however, should my beloved ever read this journal, he would soon discover my apprehension feeds off something much darker.

It has been over a month since we sailed on the SS

Majestic from Liverpool to New York. In the eight or more days it took us to cross the North Atlantic, thoughts of my mother consumed me. Stuart noticed my troubled state. Yet, for all his light-hearted talk and amusing anecdotes, his efforts remained in vain and failed to distract me. Defeat lingered in his eyes. He mentioned my mother several times. *Write to her once we have settled*, he said; *time is a great healer; she will understand once she sees you are happy. Love is a great redeemer and given time, brings forgiveness.*

Sage advice if it were that simple. But unbeknown to my husband, Helenora's rage goes far beyond a mother's wrath. She will hound me to the far reaches of this earth. Yet it is not her anger that distresses me. What I fear for the most is Stuart's safety.

I try to cast such fears from my thoughts. Dwelling on what might be does me no good. And, with that in mind, I shall endeavour to recount our journey.

The crowds of people were immense when we docked at Hudson Pier. A swarm of tired faces, hungry and afraid, and though it ailed me to witness such a mass of despair, it provided a necessary distraction. Thankfully, we passed through customs with relative ease. Our first-class tickets, good health, and Stuart's good standing as a doctor spared us the horrors of Ellis Island.

My love of the countryside has followed me throughout my life. So, to my great relief, we spent only one night in Jersey City, staying at the Royal Hotel. The hotel was well located for the Communipaw Terminal and, despite being comfortable, offered moderate prices, although I failed to see anything royal about it.

I pause here to read over my words. My comments concerning the hotel make me sound spoiled and aloof. It is not who I am. My dearest Stuart constantly says we should strive to be the best version of ourselves. It is a sentiment with which I wholeheartedly agree. I will not succumb to my mother's darkness, nor subscribe to her wicked tongue.

Mild exhaustion enabled me to sleep soundly at the Royal Hotel, strengthening me with a brighter resolve as we travelled to Washington, D.C., the following morning. We journeyed on the Royal Blue, and although the train took over five hours to reach our destination, I enjoyed the elegance and luxury of the parlour cars, especially the royal blue ceilings and matching upholstery. We dined among the panelled mahogany of the Waldorf car. If Stuart has a weakness, it is undisputedly his love for the finer things in life. He was in his element, feasting on such elaborate cuisine. Although truth be known, souped terrapins and roasted canvasback held no exquisiteness for me.

On arriving in Washington, D.C., we checked into the Willard Hotel, where we stayed for one night before boarding our last train to Richmont Cove, Virginia, our penultimate destination. I endured a fitful night's sleep. My mother's presence felt strong. But my dreams troubled me most, especially those concerning poor Mary Cowper.

Centuries have passed since Mary and I last spoke, and though I was a child at the time, she has haunted my thoughts ever since. We spent hours playing in those Welsh fields, creeping through the ferns, playing blind man's bluff at Heron Copse. Only Mary showed me compassion during those dark days following my mother's arrest. She hid me in the cellar of her parents' home. She never betrayed my trust, bringing me water and cold meats whenever she could, sitting with me in the dank silence. I was too young to question my mother. Not that such notions would ever have occurred to me. Then, and years afterwards, my mother was my world. My confidant and teacher. My saviour in many ways. A woman whose beauty and wisdom I aspired to. A woman who, for years after I lured Mary Cowper to Heron

Copse, remained my protector and showed me nothing but kindness.

At the time, both Mary and I treated it as a game. A swapping of bodies seemed mysterious and exciting. It was difficult to stop once it began. I felt Mary's and my mother's hearts beat as one; their words consumed me as the chilly midnight air carried their incantation. Then, when I stared into Mary's face, my mother's eyes looked back at me.

Only in my dreams do I hear Mary's voice; it speaks through the ravaged soul we left behind. Where have you gone? Ask the whispers. Why have you abandoned me?

The dream stayed with me all day, keeping me quiet at breakfast and holding me silent throughout the train journey to Richmont Cove. At one point, I thought I saw her out on the plains, a blur of pale light. She was lost to me again, buried beneath the dust, as the moment passed so quickly.

Upon arrival, our host, Stuart's cousin and benefactor, Dr Charles Miller, met us at the Station. He is a tall, wiry man. In his early sixties, at a guess. He was just as I pictured, from his long grey moustache and matching beard to his three-piece tweed suit. He was courteous and well-mannered, too, raising his top hat in greeting to give a glimpse of his pale bald head.

While escorting us to his buggy, Dr Miller checked his pocket watch, glancing up at the Station's clock and smiling at it assuredly. He strikes me as a man of habit. A man who likes everything to remain in its place. A man who has little tolerance for disorder and non-conformity.

Dr Miller conversed with Stuart while driving us to his home in Asherfield County. Besides inquiring about my journey and commenting on how much his wife, Clara, was looking forward to my company, he did not speak at any length with me.

March 19, 1896 -

Primrose Grange held me spellbound the moment I cast my eyes on it. Its round front tower with a conical roof, sprawling porch, and ornate wooden trim looked magnificent. Equally impressive is the interior, and once we had settled in, Mrs Miller (who insisted I call her Clara) was eager to give me a tour.

Clara is much younger than Dr Miller, and though I would never dare to ask her age, I estimate that she is barely thirty. Clara's eyes are her most striking feature, the deepest green I have seen for years. She is tall and fair-skinned, and when standing against a backdrop of morning light, her dark brown hair compliments her natural pallidness to reveal her beauty. She has shown us nothing but kindness, especially to Stuart. Not that it surprises me. With Stuart's good looks and his kind and caring nature, women often take a shine to him.

Clara began her tour with the foyer, a grand welcoming space with a winding mahogany staircase, its polished sheen reflecting the chandelier light. We then moved onto the parlour, and for all their lavishness, the blue velvet Baroque quilted sofa and gold damask wallpaper appeared somewhat abandoned owing to the inclement weather and the Millers' inability to entertain visitors. Clara seemed to acknowledge the room's neglect with a sigh. It was a brief lament, and her face quickly resumed its usual bright countenance.

After passing swiftly through the dining room, we went

to Dr Miller's study. As expected, Dr Miller has a vast number of books. They populate the shelves and cases that line the walls. Some lay open upon the large mahogany desk, while others, discarded for now, stand piled around them in small stacks. The thick, leather-bound tomes caught my eye. Secured by a locked cabinet, they stood orderly upon the shelves, gleaming through the glass panels.

Clara registered my interest with a smile. 'These are Charles's pride and joy; he sees himself as quite the antiquarian.'

'Sees himself?' I asked.

Clara blushed. 'Please forgive my churlishness. I meant no disrespect. A mere slip of the tongue. Charles *is* an antiquarian, indubitably.'

To save her further embarrassment, I asked about the tomes and their contents.

Clara remained silent at first, her hesitancy noticeable as though searching for the correct answer. 'They are a collection of texts, journals, maps, essays and old manuscripts.'

'Concerning what?'

'Why Asherfield, of course. Charles has studied its history for years. His knowledge of this area is second to one throughout the county.'

'Second to *one*?'

'Mrs Davis, Florence to her friends. She is away at the moment, visiting a sick relative. She will be back in a few weeks. No doubt you will become frequented.'

'Is she a close friend?'

Clara's eyes glowed. 'The *closest*. She is the secretary of the Asherfield Antiquarian Society. Charles is the founder and chairman, of course. However, his research would be nigh impossible without Florence's knowledge.'

'It sounds fascinating. If you would oblige, I would love to learn more. I feel such a connection with local history.'

Once again, Clara blushed. 'Alas, I have already said too much. It would infuriate Charles if I spoke out of term. Please enquire about it one night over dinner. Undoubtedly, Charles will be delighted to elaborate. He is always eager to speak about it, and if you are keen to join our little group, it would be his honour to introduce you. He can articulate it far better than I do. As Charles often reminds me, my female mind does not have the capacity.'

I felt a spiked resentment in her words but did not take her up on it.

March 23, 1896 -

AFTER ENDURING SEVERAL SLEEPLESS NIGHTS, I could muster neither the strength nor the will to write in my journal until today. My ailments are familiar ones of old. My mother, Helenora, casts her spells into the night, where the north winds carry them across the ocean. She knows not where I am. A refuge that cannot last. For now, at least, only my dreams hear her calls. Three centuries have passed since that fateful day on Heron Copse. My mother's true nature has declined throughout, but only in recent years have I noted the most significant change in her. At one time, forgiveness was no stranger to my mother's heart. Yet, since her time at Ruthin Gaol, like any other unwelcome guest, it has slowly retracted.

Darkness surmounts once you surrender to Bathin's call. My mother spent a lifetime fighting against her male persecutors. Yet, as part of Lord Bathin's recompense, she spends her life in eternal servitude. It is a paradox I have had time to ponder.

We were happy once, spending a lifetime of quiet solitude, resigned to our fate, passing willingly from one body to the next. At my mother's insistence, after every rebirth followed the remembering. It became more of a curse than a gift. There is a wretchedness to recalling every foul deed. Its dark seed flourishes after taking root, blackening the heart, and chilling the blood. It leaves you naked within, and when alone during the night's cold lament, all you long for is forgetfulness.

THANKS FOR READING

Thanks for reading. If you **enjoyed this book,** please consider leaving **a review**. Reviews make a huge difference in helping new readers find the book.

WELCOME TO HOLYHELL

'Welcome To HolyHell has the sharp plotting of peak Elmore Leonard combined with the brooding lyrical atmosphere of James Lee Burke. The characters are all marvelously well-drawn and the sense of time and place is spot on.' *Punk Noir Magazine*

'Math Bird gives us a fine bit of noir in 1976 Wales.' *Murder in Common Crime Fiction Blog*

'A remarkable work that will have you dreading as well as eagerly turning the page.' *Unlawful Acts - Crime Fiction blog*

Lies...

It's 1976, and Britain is in the grip of an unbearable heatwave when conman Bowen flees London to return to his hometown, hoping for a fresh start ... but things don't always go according to plan.

Secrets...

For young loner, Jay Ellis finding a briefcase full of cash seems the answer to all his prayers, as does the magnetic pull of the stranger, Nash, who rolls into town shortly after.

Betrayal...

Veteran conman Nash is hot on Bowen's trail to find the money stolen from him. All he has is a hunch and a newspaper clipping of the boy who witnessed his partner's death. Their fates become entwined, but in a world of violent drifters and treacherous thieves, a man's conscience can become his weakness.

A compelling, poignant and dark thriller, rich with atmosphere, for fans of small-town crime and rural noir.

Welcome to Holyhell **... where secrets can prove deadly**

HIDDEN GRACE

Revenge is best served cold, but the road to retribution starts within...

In his quest to find those who double-crossed him, Ned Flynn seeks the help of retired small-time fence, Eddie Roscoe.

But Eddie's services come with a price. If Flynn wants the information he needs, then he must help Eddie find his missing son. As Flynn and Eddie retrace the lad's steps, they discover his disappearance is more sinister than they hoped and become embroiled in a world beyond their worst nightmares.

Can Flynn and Eddie survive, or are the hunters destined to remain the prey.

The Ned Flynn Series can be enjoyed in any order.

HISTORIES OF THE DEAD
AND OTHER STORIES

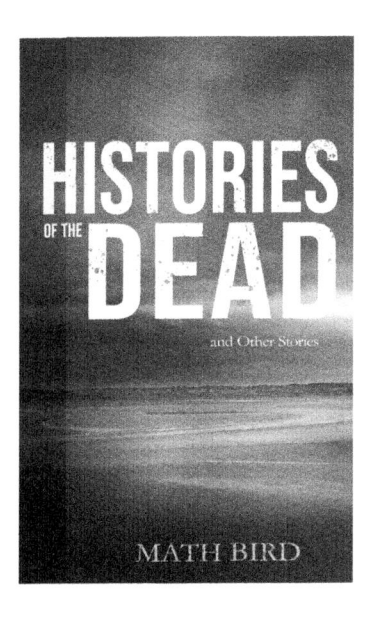

A beautiful collection of hauntingly dark crime stories.

West of the River Dee, lie the borderlands of north-east Wales, an in-between place caught between two countries.

Travel inland and you'll pass through the towns and villages, where ancient relics and abandoned factories harbour the ghosts of past glories. The tree-clad hills snake up from the valley where secrets and dark deeds whisper through the tall trees.

Whether they are fearful of the future, or worried that their best years are behind them, the characters of this striking short story collection are haunted by the past; they live on the periphery, because sometimes to live, love, or just survive, vengeance is the only option.

ABOUT THE AUTHOR

Math Bird is a British novelist and short story writer.

He's a member of the Crime Writers Association and the Horror Writers Association, and his work has aired on BBC Radio 4, BBC Radio Wales, and BBC Radio 4 Extra.

For more information:
www.mathbird.uk